ONE SIMPLE WISH

RETURN TO LIGHTHOUSE POINT

KAY CORRELL

ZURA LU PUBLISHING

Published by Zura Lu Publishing LLC

010220

Best friends.

*This book is dedicated to those special friends we have.
The ones who support us and stand by our side. The ones
who are there for us through tragedy and triumphs.
Distance and time don't matter. There's a special magic
in those extraordinary friendships.*

KAY'S BOOKS

Find more information on all my books at
kaycorrell.com

COMFORT CROSSING ~ THE SERIES

The Shop on Main - Book One

The Memory Box - Book Two

The Christmas Cottage - A Holiday Novella
(Book 2.5)

The Letter - Book Three

The Christmas Scarf - A Holiday Novella
(Book 3.5)

The Magnolia Cafe - Book Four

The Unexpected Wedding - Book Five

The Wedding in the Grove - (a crossover short

story between series - with Josephine and Paul from The Letter.)

LIGHTHOUSE POINT ~ THE SERIES
Wish Upon a Shell - Book One
Wedding on the Beach - Book Two
Love at the Lighthouse - Book Three
Cottage near the Point - Book Four
Return to the Island - Book Five
Bungalow by the Bay - Book Six

CHARMING INN ~ Return to Lighthouse Point
COMING IN 2020
One Simple Wish - Book One
Two of a Kind - Book Two
Three Little Things - Book Three
Four Short Weeks - Book Four
Five Years or So - Book Five

SWEET RIVER ~ THE SERIES
A Dream to Believe in - Book One
A Memory to Cherish - Book Two
A Song to Remember - Book Three
A Time to Forgive - Book Four
A Summer of Secrets - Book Five
A Moment in the Moonlight - Book Six

INDIGO BAY ~ A multi-author sweet romance series

Sweet Days by the Bay - Kay's Complete Collection of stories in the Indigo Bay series

Or by them separately:

Sweet Sunrise - Book Three
Sweet Holiday Memories - A short holiday story
Sweet Starlight - Book Nine

Sign up for my newsletter at my website *kaycorrell.com* to make sure you don't miss any new releases or sales.

CHAPTER 1

Sara Wren hurried out of her boss's office. If she worked the weekend, she could maybe—*maybe*—get everything finished that Diane needed. There was no way she would let her boss down now. Sara was up for a big promotion. A really big one. She might finally be made a partner at the ad agency, a position it seemed she'd been working toward her whole life.

She just had to find a new twist on the campaign for Coastal Furniture, a trendy, up-and-coming company that sold coastal-themed furniture and decorations. So far everything she'd pitched had been shot down.

She glanced at her phone. Two missed calls from Aunt Lil. She'd let them both go to voicemail. She'd have to call her back tonight when she had more time to chat. Or maybe tomorrow, since she planned on working late tonight…

She slipped into the black leather chair by her desk and spun around to look out the window. Spring was beginning to burst forth in the tiny city park that stretched out below her tenth-floor office. Not that she'd had time to enjoy the spring weather. She hadn't taken a day off in months.

It had just been a little over a year ago that she'd finally gained enough status at the agency to earn a window office. Sometimes she thought looking out that window was her only glimpse at the real world.

She sighed and turned back to her desk. Windows didn't matter. No time off didn't matter. Nothing mattered right now except figuring out the Coastal account.

She glanced up when her assistant, Rene, entered. "Hey, Sara. I took a call for you while you were in Diane's office. It sounded important. Asked that you call back as soon as possible. A Dr. Harden? You okay?"

She shrugged. "Not my doctor. Did he say what he wanted?"

"She. No, just that it was important."

She reached out and took the paper from Rene. "Thanks, I'll call her."

"Do you need anything else from me before I leave?"

Sara looked at her watch. It was already after five. "No, go home. Have a good weekend."

"But you're not going to leave for hours, are you?" Rene shook her head.

"I'll leave soon."

"But I bet you come back in tomorrow."

She grinned at Rene. "You'd be betting right. Now, go."

Rene turned and walked out the door with one parting remark. "You should really take a day off sometime."

Rene was right. She should. But not this weekend.

She picked up the paper and dialed this mysterious Dr. Harden. She ended up talking to some woman, who asked her to hold. She drummed her fingers on the desk and glanced at her watch. She really didn't have time to wait for the doctor to get to the phone. She'd give her two more minutes, then she'd hang up. The doctor could just track her down again.

"Ms. Wren? Sara Wren? Lillian Charm's niece?" A female voice came across the airwaves.

"Yes. I got a message you called."

"I'm Dr. Harden, from Memorial Hospital on Belle Island."

Her heart skipped a beat. Belle Island?

"I have some bad news, I'm afraid."

Sara willed her to stop. To not say another word. To—

"It's your Aunt Lillian."

"Is she hurt?" Her voice was low, hoping it was something minor. But then why wasn't it Aunt Lillian calling her?

Guilt rushed through her. Aunt Lil *had* called. *Twice.* She hadn't even taken the time to check the messages.

She steadied herself by placing a hand on the edge of the desk.

"I'm afraid Lillian took a bad fall late last night." Her voice was caring but held an efficient clip to it.

"How bad?" She held her breath.

"She just got out of surgery. Broken hip and injured her arm. She's still a bit out of it from the anesthesia and some pain meds now, but she insisted I call you after the surgery. She said she'd left you messages but hadn't told you what happened. Didn't want to leave it in a message."

She couldn't imagine her perky, energetic aunt with all these injuries. She swore Aunt Lillian had more energy than she did.

"We've given her some pretty strong meds. She's in a lot of pain."

"Tell her I'll be there as soon as possible. I'll get the early morning flight out." As if rushing there now would assuage her guilt over not picking up the phone when Aunt Lil had called today. When Aunt Lil had *needed* her.

She hung up the phone and pushed back from the desk. She stood and looked at the people hurrying along the street below her. Hurrying home to their families. People who needed them. Like Aunt Lil needed her.

She turned away from the window and squared her shoulders. Now she needed to march back into Diane's office and tell her she had to leave and go back to Belle Island.

Sara walked back into her boss's office. Diane glanced up. "You had another question?" Her voice was annoyed with the interruption.

"I—I need a few days off."

"When?"

"Now. I'm leaving in the morning. First thing." Sara gulped in a deep breath and continued. "I need to go to Belle Island, Florida. My aunt is hurt. She took a bad fall." She rushed on, trying to explain. "She doesn't have anyone else but me. I need to go help her."

"Well, the timing is inconvenient."

Typical Diane remark.

Sara didn't even give a reply to that. Like her aunt picked this very time to fall to inconvenience Diane. She gritted her teeth. This was not the time to cross Diane. If she got the promotion, they'd be equals. Or almost equals. Partners. She could push back then, or take a stand. But not now.

"But we have one last chance at another presentation for Coastal Furniture. It's in a few days. Our *last* shot." Diane frowned.

"I'm afraid I won't be here for it." She squared her shoulders against what she knew was coming.

"You have to be." Diane shook her head.

"I can't. I can still work on it while I'm back home. I'll give you all my notes and presentation slides. You could give the presentation. Or, if you could push it back a bit…"

Diane sat and stared at her, a deep frown crossing her face. Then she sighed. "I feel like you'd do a better job presenting your concept. I'll see if I can push it back. You'll be back in a few days, right?"

"I'm just not sure, yet. I need to get there and see how she is."

"After you get there, call me and let me know when you think you'll be getting back. I can call you with questions, right?"

"Of course." Sara nodded.

"Good. Keep in touch." Diane bent her head over her work and Sara knew that was her dismissal.

She walked out the door and down the hallway to her office, sinking onto her chair and glancing at the work piled on her desk. She was going to get so behind.

CHAPTER 2

Sara sat quietly beside her aunt's hospital bed. The nurse had said Aunt Lil had been given some pain meds, and Sara didn't want to disturb her. She could see the creases on her aunt's face, even in her sleep. Aunt Lil moaned slightly.

Sara took her hand and squeezed it. "I'm here for you," she whispered softly.

She looked up as the door opened, frowning at the interruption until she saw it was Robin.

She quickly got up, crossed the room, and Robin threw her arms around her in a quick hug.

"Hey, you." Robin whispered the words.

"Oh, it's so great to see you." Sara kept her voice low and clasped Robin's hands in hers.

"I heard about Lil and figured you'd come. How's she doing?"

"I think she's in a lot of pain. She's pretty out of it right now."

"Sara, is that you?" Her aunt's weak voice crossed the room.

She turned and hurried back beside the bed. "I'm here." She brushed Aunt Lil's hair away from her face and leaned over to kiss her cheek.

"I didn't mean to pull you away from work."

"Don't be silly. It's okay. There's nowhere else I would want to be."

Robin came to stand beside her. "Hey, Lil. You gave us quite a scare."

"I'm sorry." Aunt Lil closed her eyes.

"Just glad they got you all taken care of." Robin glanced over at the machines beside the bed.

"I think she fell back to sleep." Sara placed her hands on the railing of the bed, holding on for support. Aunt Lil was the strong one, her rock. It was hard to process that this frail woman was her vibrant aunt.

"That's what she needs now. Rest." Robin looked at her. "And you need a meal."

"No, I don't want to leave her. What if she wakes up again?"

"Okay, I'll head to Magic Cafe and grab you a meal."

"I'm not hungry."

"But you'll eat. You look exhausted and you've lost a lot of weight since I last saw you."

"I've been… busy." Too busy to come back home to visit her aunt. Too busy to keep in touch with her best friends. All engrossed in her career. The guilt swept through her again, smothering her with remorse.

"Well, I'm bringing you food. Need anything else?"

"No."

"Okay, I'll be back soon." Robin disappeared out the door.

She settled into the chair beside the bed and stared at the rise and fall of Aunt Lil's chest with her ragged breaths.

She finally leaned back and grabbed her laptop. Might as well get some work done while she sat there.

"Good morning, dear." Aunt Lil's voice drifted into her consciousness.

Sara opened her eyes and looked around, trying to remember where she was.

Ah, the hospital.

Sunshine streamed in the window. She stretched, trying to get the kink out of her back from sleeping in the hospital chair all night. She stood, leaned over, and kissed her aunt. "You're awake."

"I am. I think they're giving me some powerful pain meds. I dreamed you were here. Then when I woke up this morning, I saw you were. When did you get here?"

"Yesterday."

"It's good to see you." Her aunt smiled weakly. "Sorry to be such trouble."

"You are never any trouble."

"I've made a mess of things this time. I mean, the inn won't run itself. Jay can run it for a few days, but he can't manage it and cook and do everything. Plus we just lost a worker this week. She quit without notice."

The Charming Inn and Cottages—named after her aunt, Lillian Charm—and her aunt's pride and joy. The inn was right on the beach and surrounded by small cottages. Busy season was coming up. No wonder Aunt Lil was worried. "Jay's still working for you?"

"Sure is. Don't know what I'd do without him. And you should see our dining room now. We expanded and get quite a business from locals and tourists along with our guests. We're open for dinner now, too. Not just breakfast."

"Really?" She realized, once again, it had been way too long since she'd been back to the island. "Well, don't worry about it. You just rest and get better. I'll head over to the inn and check on things. I can help out for a bit."

"Are you sure? I know you've been so busy at work."

"I can work from here and I'll help at the inn."

"That's a lot to ask." Her aunt shook her head.

"And yet, you didn't ask. I offered." Like she wouldn't do anything in the whole world for her aunt. She owed her so much.

"Then, thank you."

"You're welcome." She smiled as she saw some of the frown lines ease on her aunt's face.

"Now, why don't you run to the inn and get cleaned up? Your room is still there waiting for you. I know I've talked about converting our little wing of the inn into guest rooms. But... I've just never done it. I kind of like having our own little area to ourselves. Remember when you named it The Nest?

The Nest. Their perfect little world. Their own private area off to one side of the inn. No, she hadn't forgotten it.

Aunt Lil leaned back against the pillows. "Why don't you grab a shower and change clothes?"

She looked down at her wrinkled outfit. "That's probably a good idea. I'll do that. I'll check in on things, then come back to visit you."

"I think I might just take another little nap."

"Good idea." She kissed her aunt's cheek and gathered her things. A shower did sound like a great idea.

She headed out of the hospital, into the fresh air and sunshine. She sucked in the fresh, salty air. So nice after the stifling hospital air. As she crossed the parking lot, she dug around in her purse, looking for her keys. The sound of an ambulance caught her attention and she looked back toward the hospital.

As she glanced across the parking lot, she swore the man standing by the front of the hospital looked amazingly like—

But that was silly. He wouldn't be here. He

was off in some big city making a living. Probably already a partner at some big prestigious ad agency. That had always been his plan.

That had been her plan, too. And she was *almost* there.

She triumphantly found her keys, waving them in glee, and opened the car door. Shower time. Then coffee. She needed coffee.

Noah McNeil stood on the sidewalk outside the hospital almost hidden behind one of the pillars.

He'd always known there was a chance he might see Sara again, but she hadn't been here in years, and he'd avoided her the one time she'd come back to visit her aunt.

No one in town was even aware he knew Sara.

But, of course, she'd come back now that Lil had taken that fall. Everyone on Belle Island knew she'd fallen. He looked down at the flowers he clutched in his hand. He was on his way into the hospital to drop them off for one of his employees who'd had minor surgery. But he made no move to enter the hospital. Instead he stood and watched Sara.

She stood in the parking lot, blinking against the bright morning sun. Her brown hair lay tousled about her shoulders, and she was digging in her purse.

A quick smile crossed his face. He remembered that quirk of hers. She was forever digging around in her huge purses, looking for something. She was so organized about some things, but not those big purses she loved to carry.

Noah knew he should *probably* just walk right up to her and say how sorry he was about her aunt's accident, but the timing just didn't seem right. What could he say after all these years?

And besides, she'd made it clear what her choice was all those years ago back in Boston. Not that he blamed her.

And he wouldn't have done things differently, either. He'd made his own choice back then. He knew that and wouldn't change a thing.

She took out a set of keys with a triumphant flourish and walked the last distance to her car. He watched her every step.

She glanced back his direction and he quickly stepped behind the pillar again.

No, this wasn't the right time to talk to her. Not after all this time.

Besides, if he went up to her now, he'd have to explain why he was here on the island...

And that was really her fault, too.

CHAPTER 3

Sara pulled her car onto the crushed shell drive that led to the back wing of the inn with its own private entrance. She tried to figure out the last time she'd been here. It had been a year or so. Okay, maybe more. Lots more. Her aunt had come to visit her in Boston, though. And they talked on the phone all the time. Or they used to. She'd gotten so busy at work that their phone calls had tapered off.

Guilt washed over her. She should have come back more often. Her aunt had given up everything for her, and how had she repaid her? By being too busy to visit.

She looked at the familiar, large, rambling inn. The outside of it was in wonderful shape, as always. Her aunt took meticulous care of the place, always renovating the rooms to keep them updated. The cheerful shade of light yellow paint on the inn was barely weathered from the salty air.

She slid out of the car, grabbed her bags, and climbed the steps to the back door. She used her key to enter The Nest. The same key she'd had since she'd come to live with Aunt Lil as a young child. She could have gone in the front of the inn, but she loved coming in the back way. More cozy and just Aunt Lil's and her area.

Memories attacked her as she stepped inside and looked around the wide, open space. Her aunt's collection of lighthouse statues and carvings along the shelf to the left. Photos of Aunt Lil and her on the beach in frames of every shade of teal, her aunt's favorite color. She crossed over and picked up a photo, tracing her finger over her aunt's face. She set it down and picked up a photo of her mother and Aunt Lil when they were in high school. They almost looked like twins, though they were two years apart.

She set the photo down, walked over to the couch, and grabbed the worn teal wrap hanging off the back. Taking a deep breath, she inhaled the scent. It smelled of Aunt Lil, The Nest, the salty air... everything she loved about the island. With a sigh, she set the wrap back on the couch, grabbed her things, and headed down the hall to her bedroom.

She looked around the room. Not much had changed since she'd lived here. The old posters were down and rolled up in a corner, though. The same bedspread and her dresser with a music box on top. She opened the box and smiled as the familiar tune drifted across the room in tinkling, metallic tones.

She opened the blinds to let in the sunlight. She loved this inn. Why had she stayed away so long?

She stretched her arms and turned around to unpack. She was exhausted and hoped a quick shower would revive her. She'd been so tired that for a moment, back at the hospital, she thought she'd seen Noah McNeil.

Which was ridiculous.

Yes, she must be overly tired.

Sara quickly took her shower, then headed into

the main part of the inn. The place looked exactly the same. Cheerful teal lettering on the large sign behind the reception desk said welcome. Large windows stretched across the front, peeking out to the Adirondack chairs spread across the long front porch. The large wooden double door with who knew how many coats of paint on it.

How many afternoons had she spent here after school either doing homework or later helping her aunt? So many great memories. Her aunt always plopped her down wherever she was working at the time.

The door swung open and Sara glanced at the woman standing there in the sunlight spilling through the doorway. "Tally?"

Tally looked at her in surprise. "Sara, you're here. Oh, I'm so sorry about Lil." Tally walked up to her and gave her a hug. "I hope she's up and feeling better soon. I hear it was quite the fall. If there's anything I can do, you let me know."

"Thanks, Tally. I appreciate that."

"I was just dropping by to see if Jay had any updates on Lil or needed anything."

"She's in a lot of pain. Sleeping a lot."

"I'm sure she'll be better in no time. She's a feisty one, that Lil."

"She is that." Sara nodded.

"And you come by Magic Cafe while you're here and get a meal. We'll catch up. I feel like I haven't seen you in forever."

Tally and her aunt both owned restaurants on Belle Island—though her aunt's was a small dining room compared to Tally's Magic Cafe— but they were friendly competitors and often helped each other out. Such were the townspeople here on the island. She'd missed that. Everyone seemed to be not-so-friendly competitors in Boston. Really, more like cutthroat competitors.

"I will come by." She nodded. She would try. She would.

Tally had welcomed her from the first day she'd come to the island to live with her aunt. Frightened. Not knowing what was happening.

One day she'd been at home with the babysitter while her dad took her mom up in his plane. They'd loved to get away and go flying for a few hours. Then the next thing the police had been at the door, then the next day Aunt Lil had come. And soon after that, her things had been packed up in a handful of suitcases and boxes and she'd moved to Belle Island to live with her aunt.

"You going to help out your aunt with the inn while she's out of commission?"

"I'm going to try."

"Jay can help you. He's a smart man. Been here with Lil for a long time. I'm sure you two can work it out."

"I hope so. I mean I grew up working here, and sometimes helped cook, but I know nothing about running an inn."

"Well, the offer stands. I'll help in any way I can. And Susan will help, too, I'm sure."

She looked at Tally and must have looked confused.

"Susan took over running her brother's inn, Belle Island Inn."

She vaguely remembered her aunt telling her that someone had taken over running Belle Island Inn. She nodded. "Thanks." Yet another competitor willing to help.

"I better run. Just wanted to hear how Lil was doing. And the offer stands. Come by Magic Cafe." Tally headed out the door and Sara made for the dining room and the craved cup of coffee.

She paused at the entryway, amazed by the

changes. The dining area was twice the size it had been. It looked like Lil had taken out the wall between the dining area and the large storage room and extended the room out farther toward the beach so that an alcove of tables had a wonderful view of the water.

She was immediately met with the aroma of fresh-brewed coffee. Exactly what she needed. She crossed over to the counter at one side of the room and started to grab some from the coffeepot.

"Hey, I usually serve the customers."

She spun around. "Hey, Jay." He looked exactly the same. Tall, lean, sandy blonde hair in need of a haircut, and a t-shirt that said *I Cook, Therefore You Eat*. He never disappointed. There was always a t-shirt with some kind of saying on it. She smiled.

"Sara?"

"Yep. It's me."

"Been a long time."

She wished everyone would quit reminding her how long it had been since she'd been home. "I came as soon as I heard about Aunt Lil."

"How's she doing? I dropped by the night she had surgery, but she was out of it. Besides, I kind of have my hands full here. Want to keep things running smoothly while she's out of commission."

"And I'm here to help."

He looked at her skeptically. "Really?"

"Yes, I promised Aunt Lil."

"I'm sure not going to turn down any help." He waved to some new customers coming in and motioned for them to sit anywhere.

"Here, I'll get them." She eyed the cup of coffee she'd just poured.

He laughed. "Drink your coffee. The breakfast crowd is slowing down."

She gratefully clasped the cup of coffee and went to the small office her aunt had at the back of the inn. Collapsing into the desk chair, she stared at the pile of papers on the worn desk. She riffled through the pages. Orders in one pile. Bills in another. Her aunt's business checkbook sprawled across the desk. Did Aunt Lil still write checks for everything? No online banking?

Her phone beeped and she looked at it. A text from Diane with a handful of questions. Ones that were answered if Diane would carefully read the report she'd given her. She typed in the answers, leaving out the snarky remark to just check the file.

She set the phone on the desk and took a sip of the coffee, trying not to despair. Somehow she was going to have to figure all this out *and* keep Diane happy *and* come up with a campaign for Coastal Furniture?

CHAPTER 4

J ay finally chased Sara away about six, saying it was a slow evening. She went to the hospital to check on Aunt Lil, but she was sound asleep, so she drove back to The Nest and sank onto the couch, grateful to be off her feet. She'd forgotten how tiring it was working at the inn. She'd worked the front desk for a while, handled some guests' problems, and helped serve the beginning of the dinner crowd.

She glanced over to the photos, got up, and picked up a photo of Aunt Lil standing outside the inn.

"Oh, Aunt Lil, what am I going to do? I don't know a thing about running your inn, but I can't let you down."

A quick double-knock at the back door grabbed her attention, and she put the photo carefully back in place. Before she could cross to answer the door, it swung wide open.

Robin swept into the room. "I figured you'd need some moral support. Heard you worked at the inn today."

"I did. I'm exhausted."

"You look horrible." Robin grinned.

She shoved a rebellious lock of hair from her face. "Gee, thanks. I told Aunt Lil I'd help, but what do I know about the business side of things?"

"I'm here to help. Anything and everything. What can I do for you?"

"I don't even know where to start…"

"I tell you what. It's getting late. I'm going to raid Lil's stash of wine… you know she always has a nice bottle of red around here somewhere. We're going to go out on the deck and watch the sunset. Tomorrow we'll deal with the inn."

There were no words for how grateful she was for the support. She let Robin pour them wine and lead her out onto the deck. She took a deep breath of the salty air. She'd get through this, she would. But thank goodness for Robin's help. And Jay's.

They settled onto the wooden chairs lining the private deck tucked to the side of The Nest with an amazing view of the sea. Robin handed her a glass. Slowly the sound of the waves and their mesmerizing march to the shore soothed her. She glanced down the beach toward Lighthouse Point. She had to make time to go walk down there. The lighthouse had always been a touchstone to her. An anchor in her life. A constant watching over her.

"There you are."

She turned to see Charlotte standing at the stairs at the end of the deck.

"I thought I'd find you out here."

"Char." She jumped up and hurried over to her friend. Charlotte threw her arms around her. "What are you doing here?"

"Heard about Lil and that you were actually here in town. Thought I'd come visit."

"All the way from California?"

"Yep, made plans to come as soon as Robin called me." Charlotte looked at them and eyed their glasses of wine. "Hey, you started without me. I'm going to go grab a glass and join you."

She came back out, filled her glass, and sat beside them. "How's Lil doing?"

"She's still pretty out of it. Dropped by to see her tonight, but she was sleeping."

"So how long until she's up and about?" Charlotte looked at her. "You going to stay until she's all recovered?"

That's Charlotte. Always direct and to the point.

"I'm not sure how long I can stay. I'm going to try and work remotely, but I don't know how long I can do that."

"Who's running the inn?" Charlotte took a sip of wine.

"Me?" She shrugged.

Robin laughed. "Sara offered to help out, but she's in over her head with everything. I offered to help her."

"I could help," Charlotte offered.

"But your painting... I thought you had that gallery show coming up."

"That... didn't pan out." She shook her head and looked out at the water. "I could stay here a bit. I miss the island. I miss you two."

"I'm not going to turn down any help that's offered, that's for sure. Busy season is coming and Aunt Lil is already short a worker she said. I need to find her more help and figure out stuff like ordering and paying bills and… well, everything."

"I'm your girl." Charlotte tapped her chest with her finger. "Haven't worked at the inn since high school, but I bet I can manage."

Somehow she couldn't picture Charlotte waiting tables in the expanded dining room or cleaning the cottages, but who was she to turn away help?

"Then you should stay here with me at the inn while you're here. We're not full yet. I'll get you a room."

Charlotte grinned. "I was hoping you'd offer."

"Perfect, then it's settled." She leaned back in the chair and took a sip of the wine. The mild night air swirled around her, stirring up memories, reminding her how much she'd missed the island.

"I'm so glad you two are here." She almost choked on the words. She was so grateful to have her friends with her, by her side. Everything seemed *almost* normal sitting here with them.

"No other place I'd be." Robin's lips curved in a quick smile.

"Me either," Charlotte agreed.

They sat in silence and watched the sunset explode across the sky in brilliant oranges and purples.

"The three of us back together again, just like old times," Robin said softly. "I'm just sorry it took Lil's accident to make it happen."

CHAPTER 5

Sara dropped in to see Aunt Lil the next morning after the breakfast rush at the inn. She had to hurry back soon, though, to meet up with Robin and Charlotte. They'd promised her they'd conquer the inn and get things running smoothly.

"Sara, dear. There you are." Aunt Lil was sitting up in bed eating a bit of late breakfast. That was an improvement.

"Good morning. Glad to see you up this morning."

"I told them they had to cut back on the pain meds. They were just knocking me out. That's no way to live."

"But are you in pain?" She scanned her aunt's face for any signs.

"It's manageable."

"Don't act too tough. You need time to heal."

Aunt Lil frowned. "About that. The doctor came in early this morning and we had a talk. Well, she talked. I argued."

"What did she say?"

"She thinks in a few days it would be best for me to go to a rehab place on the mainland. I need daily physical therapy and time to get my strength back."

"You should listen to her."

"I told her I could get stronger at home, but there is the daily physical therapy thing she insists I need."

"Then you'll go to the rehab place and get stronger," she insisted.

Her aunt sighed. "But the inn and the busy season coming... oh, and did Jay tell you we're in the middle of renovating two cottages and they have to get finished? We have them almost fully booked for the season. Well, at least one of them."

No, Jay hadn't told her that. He was probably afraid she'd run screaming back to Boston. "All of which I have under control." Just a tiny exaggeration. She hopefully *would* after Robin and Charlotte helped her out.

"It's too much for you to do. And your job…"

"I'm working remotely." As if to taunt her, her phone beeped. She glanced at it, then slipped it back in her purse. Diane could wait a few minutes for her answer.

"Are you sure? I don't want to be a bother. We could close the inn for a few weeks or so."

"Not a chance. Busy season is starting. I know you said you earn more than half your income at the inn during the busy season."

"I do, but—"

"No buts. I'm going to stay and keep things going."

"You know, dear, you don't owe me anything." Her aunt looked directly at her.

"I owe you *everything*. I don't know what I would have done without you. But that has nothing to do with this. I want to help you."

"You're certain?"

"I am. Besides, it will be a nice break for me." Okay, that was a bit of a white lie, but if it helped relieve Aunt Lil's guilt, she was okay with bending the truth a bit. "And guess what?

Charlotte came to town for a visit. She and Robin are going to help out at the inn."

"Oh, that's wonderful. Tell Charlotte to stop by here and say hi. I haven't seen her in a long time."

Neither had she, and that was just wrong. Best friends should keep in touch better, see each other more often. She always blamed it on how busy she was at work, but to be honest, that had been her choice. She was so intent on landing the promotion.

"I'll tell her to stop by before you head to rehab. I'm sure she'd love to catch up with you."

Aunt Lil had practically been an aunt to all three of them. From the early school years when Sara had moved here all the way through high school. Robin and Charlotte loved Aunt Lil as much as she did.

"I better head to the inn. I'm meeting Char and Robin. We're going to get everything organized. Don't worry about a thing."

"You call me if you have any questions at all. Any. And Jay knows a lot about everything, too."

"We'll be fine." She hoped they'd be fine...

She probably shouldn't have insisted that they'd be fine.

"Sara, there you are." Jay stood in the kitchen at the inn, a mop in his hands. "The dishwasher broke. Well, more than broke. It leaked all over the floor. I have that cleaned up. Mostly. But we'll have to wash the dishes by hand until I get a chance to look at it. I'll try to see if I can fix it after breakfast."

Jay's t-shirt proclaimed *It's a Golden Day*, with a bright, smiling sun on it.

Ha. As if.

"So Robin and Charlotte are coming by to help this morning."

"Robin is already here." Jay nodded in the direction of the office. "She came in early this morning."

She frowned. "She did? What about her job? I thought she'd go in there to work, then come here later."

Jay shrugged. "No clue, but she's here now. She's an early riser, anyway."

She looked at him. How did he know that Robin was always up early? When had he and Robin become friends? She thought they were just barely acquaintances. Of course, a lot had changed since the last time she'd been to town.

She grabbed a cup of coffee and headed to the office. "Morning. Jay said you'd already been here for a while."

"Just a bit." Robin looked up from the desk. "Jay gave me a list of things that need to be ordered, and I'm looking at old files to see where Lil orders things from. I've got a good list going. Want me to just order them for you?"

"Yes, that would be great." She frowned. "Did you know two of the cottages are being renovated? I'm going to have to go check them out and see what's left to be done."

"Yes, Jay said they were working on two cottages."

Sara looked at her friend. "So Jay told you, but not me?"

Robin laughed. "We were trying to find the right time to tell you."

She grinned. "Good choice. I think if I'd heard that the first day, I would have... well, it doesn't matter. It's work that needs to be done."

"What time do you think Charlotte will show up?" Robin leaned back in the desk chair and stretched.

"Oh, about noon. You know how she hates morning. Plus the time change from California to here."

"I know. She kept wanting to stay up last night because it was early to her, but I was so tired and had to tag out." Robin shuffled some papers on the desk.

"Yes, we stayed up talking for another hour after you left until I was ready to drop from exhaustion."

"Maybe we should wake her up early so she doesn't keep us up so late." Robin grinned.

"You can try that, but I'm not. I've seen Charlotte when she gets up too early."

CHAPTER 6

That afternoon Jay showed Sara, Robin, and Charlotte the cottages Aunt Lil was remodeling.

"This one and the one next to it. There's still lots left to do." Jay opened the door to the teal cottage. Aunt Lil had named each cottage by the color of their brightly painted doors. This one was her favorite, of course, because of the teal.

Sara stepped inside and looked around. No furniture, no window treatments and the walls in need of a fresh coat of paint.

Jay turned around. "I did get all the plumbing updated. New tile in the bathroom with new cabinets and counters."

"Where's all the furniture?" Charlotte asked.

Jay scrubbed a hand over his face. "New beds and mattresses were ordered. They're stored in the bedroom of the yellow cottage. Oh, and nightstands."

"I think I saw an order for lamps in the stack of papers I went through. I'll check when I get back to the office." Robin wandered over to the large picture windows. "We'll need some window treatments."

"Lil had blinds in here before. They were yellowed a bit, so she wanted new ones. If you get some, I can hang them for you," Jay offered.

"I'll measure for them and order them." She could at least do that much.

"The rooms all have a couple of side chairs and small tables, too. The ones in here before were pretty beat up so she got rid of them." Jay frowned. "Lil usually goes to flea markets and antique shops and buys those. Then she paints them with some chalk stuff."

"Chalk paint?" Charlotte's eyes lit up.

"Maybe?" Jay shrugged.

"I could do that. I love to paint furniture." Charlotte turned to her. "Let me do that for you. I'll go out to find the pieces and I'll paint them."

"I'm not going to turn you down. That sounds great. I know nothing about painting furniture."

"I'll do shades of teal for this cottage, and shades of yellow for the yellow cottage. It will look great. I promise."

Sara didn't doubt it for a moment. Charlotte was crazy talented with all things artsy.

"I usually do the painting of the walls, too. But I'm a bit busy without Lil here." Jay looked around the room.

"We'll help paint," Robin offered.

"I've never painted a wall in my life." She looked at the faded walls. How hard could it be to paint them, though, right?

"Not a problem. We'll show you how." Charlotte grinned. "Looks like I have a lot of painting in my future."

"At least the tile floors are still in good shape." Sara looked at the floors, grateful that they at least were still useable.

"Lil wanted the grout cleaned on them."

Of course, she did. Lil liked everything kept in perfect shape. "Okay, we'll figure that out, too."

Jay laughed. "I can do that."

"What would we do without you, Jay?" Robin grinned at him.

He tossed her a lazy grin back. "I don't know. I'm kind of the perfect guy to have around, aren't I? All-around handyman and as a bonus, a cook."

Sara watched the exchange between Jay and Robin.

Hm...

"If I could borrow the inn's van, I'll head out now and see what furniture I can find," Charlotte offered. "And I could pick up the wall paint."

"Of course you can use the van. Do you need any help?" Sara didn't know where she was most needed. And as if to taunt her, her phone beeped again. Another text from Diane.

"I'll go with Charlotte. You answer your boss. That's her again, isn't it?" Robin looked at her pointedly. "She texts a million times a day."

"She does. But I really should answer this one, then finish up the proposal for her."

"Okay, then. You do your work-work. Char and I will go shop. Let's go." Robin walked out of the cottage.

They all followed her out the door because no one ever argued with Robin.

Noah McNeil got up from his desk and stretched. He'd been here since early morning and had worked right through lunch, though that was typical of his days. Today they'd had a senior luncheon at the community center and tonight was the dress rehearsal for the youth play that was opening this weekend.

His job as director of the community center was a busy one, but then he loved keeping busy now that Zoe was gone. He missed her and hadn't fully adjusted to life without her here. Nothing quite filled that empty space.

He pushed away his thoughts of loneliness. He really should consider getting a quick bite to eat. He wanted to stay and watch the dress rehearsal even though he probably wouldn't be needed. He'd normally head to the dining room at Charming Inn since it was just a quick walk from the community center, but he didn't want to chance running into Sara again like he had yesterday.

Not that he'd actually *run* into her.

More like hidden from her.

He would see her sometime. Rumor around the island was that she was staying here for a while to help Lil. But he wanted it to be on his terms.

He wanted to be prepared for it.

He wanted to figure out what the heck he was going to say to her...

CHAPTER 7

Sara didn't sleep well that night. Early in the morning, she finally gave up and got out of bed, dressing quickly so she could walk out to Lighthouse Point to see the sunrise. Well, the reflected sunrise since she'd be facing west. But usually, the point didn't disappoint.

She stepped outside, paused, and turned back. She slipped her cell phone out of her pocket and hurried back inside to leave it on the counter. A brief walk and a respite from Diane's inevitable texts wouldn't hurt anything, would it? She didn't want the beeping phone to disturb the peace of the morning. While she was at it, she kicked off her shoes. Barefoot was always better. Nothing better than the feel of the soft sand beneath her feet.

The sky was just beginning to lighten as she crossed over to walk at the water's edge. The waves were barely rolling in this morning. It amazed her that the gulf could almost look like a gigantic lake on some still mornings. A lone seagull flew by, then a flock of pelicans.

She headed up the beach to the lighthouse. When she got there, she walked right up to it and touched its well-worn brick exterior. "Hello, old friend. I've missed you." Silly, but true.

She crossed the sand and walked near the water. She hadn't ever really believed in the town's legend that said if you make a wish at Lighthouse Point and throw a shell into the ocean, your wish would come true. That was silly. Nonsense. Just a ridiculous myth.

She eyed one shell that seemed to call to her.

Nah, that was silly.

She sank onto the sand and watched while the clouds over the sea began to brighten with rosy shades of delicate pinks reflected from the sunrise behind her. The fresh sea air filled her lungs. It was so nice to just sit and do nothing. When was the last time she'd done that?

She did feel a tiny bit guilty about leaving her cell phone back at the inn. But just a tiny bit.

Noah took Cooper for a walk on the beach early most mornings. He felt bad that Cooper was stuck home alone while he worked most days, though he did try and bring him to the community center when he could. The old Australian shepherd was getting grey around the face and had lost some of the boundless energy he used to have, but he still adored his morning walks on the beach.

They headed across the sand, Cooper running in front of him to chase a bird. A game he played but never really worked hard at winning. Coop trotted back toward him.

Most mornings, if they had time, they went all the way to the lighthouse and back home. He glanced at his watch. They had time today.

He walked at the water's edge, watching the sky brighten. The air was still cool, but he knew it would heat up soon and the humidity would crash down around them. But for now, it was perfect.

He missed Zoe tagging along beside him in the mornings when she'd lived with him. But, like all things, she'd moved on. He was happy for her, he was. But he missed her. This year had been a big adjustment when she'd moved away and taken a new job near Orlando.

A lone person sat on the beach in front of the lighthouse. Another early morning walker who'd probably paused to watch the sunrise. He briefly considered turning around and leaving them to their solitude, but Cooper had run ahead of him.

He hurried after the dog, hoping the beach sitter liked overly friendly dogs.

"Cooper, come here," he called out, but Cooper either didn't hear or ignored him.

He walked closer to the woman who had her arms wrapped around the dog, laughing as he licked her.

Good, at least she was a dog lover.

She looked up at him and he froze.

"Noah." She knew she'd said his name but wondered if he'd heard it. Her voice was a whisper, barely audible over the gentle lap of the waves.

"Ah... um... Sara." He stared at her.

She loosened her hold on the dog and

climbed to her feet. The dog bounded over to Noah.

Noah.

Noah here on Belle Island.

"I see you've met Cooper."

"Yes. What?" She paused, confused. "What are you doing here?" Here on *her* island.

"Cooper and I are out for a walk."

"I can see that. But why are you *here?*"

He paused for a moment then swept his arm wide. "I live here."

"Here? On the island?" He wasn't making any sense. She stared at him standing there, looking just as handsome as ever, but in a more relaxed way. His tanned face and the easy way he ruffled his dog's head were a bit incongruent with the precisely dressed, hard-driven coworker she'd known him as. *And* they'd often said neither of them would ever own a pet because they were too busy with work. Look at him now all friendly with his dog.

Clearly a *pet.*

"I moved here quite a few years ago."

"Here?" She knew she was repeating herself, but why was he *here?* Her heart hammered in her chest, and she struggled to breathe.

He shifted his feet in the sand, petted

Cooper again—his *dog*—then looked back at her. "I... you... well, you were always talking about Belle Island back when—you know— when we were dating. It sounded like a wonderful place, so unlike the city." He looked out at the sea, then back at her. "There came a time I needed a bit of a break. I decided to come here and see what it was like. I mean you talked nonstop about how wonderful it was. I admit I fell in love with the island immediately."

She frowned, processing his words. "So you just... moved here?"

"I did. Went back to Philadelphia where I was living. Quit my job. Moved here."

"There isn't much need for a big ad agency here on the island. What do you do here?"

"I run the community center."

He might as well have told her he ran the zoo. A community center manager? He'd been all business first and obviously just as cutthroat as everyone else at their ad agency.

... along with being a sore loser when she got the promotion they had both been up for. Because he'd left without a word. He hadn't been the man she'd thought he was.

She shook her head to clear her thoughts. All that didn't matter now. But Noah being on the island was a complication she didn't need right now. She wanted to stomp her feet like a toddler and have a tantrum and yell at him that Belle Island was *hers*, not his. But she couldn't do that.

But she *wanted* to.

"I heard about Lil. That's a tough deal for her. I hope she heals quickly."

"You know Aunt Lil?" But, of course, if he *lived* here on the island he'd know her. Everyone did.

"I do. She's a great lady."

"Does she know who *you* are?"

"She knows me." He neatly sidestepped the question.

"But does she know about you and me? Us?"

"By the time I moved here, there was no us."

No kidding. Because he'd just up and disappeared without a word. But she refused to ask him about it. She had some pride left.

"I better get back to the inn." She paused, not that she owed him any explanation. "I'm helping Aunt Lil out at the inn for a bit."

He just nodded.

She took one last look at his tan, chiseled

face with a hint of a scruffy beard—that would have never happened back at the agency—and turned away from him. She hurried off down the beach, controlling her steps so it didn't look like she was actually *running* away from him. She only allowed herself one quick glance back over her shoulder.

Noah and Cooper stood at the edge of the water watching her scurry away.

"Well, that was awkward, wasn't it, Coop?"

The Aussie just looked up at him and wagged his tail. He'd been lucky to find an Australian shepherd with a tail. Most had their tails docked. Well, it was *usually* lucky. Sometimes Cooper used it to sweep everything off his coffee table in his exuberance.

"You had to choose that particular woman to go up to and love on, didn't you?" He shook his head.

Sara got smaller and smaller in the distance as she hurried down the beach. She'd looked even better in person up close than she'd looked across the parking lot the other day. Though, her eyes looked tired. Not surprising with worrying about her aunt.

Somehow he couldn't imagine the hard-driven, climb-the-ladder coworker running her aunt's inn. And how in the world had she gotten the time off of work? She was still with the same agency they'd both worked for. He admitted he'd looked her up from time to time on the internet. Not creepily. He just wondered how she was doing.

That agency was not known for giving workers personal time, and most of the up-and-coming employees rarely even took their vacation.

Yet, here she was on Belle Island, helping her aunt.

He didn't know why she was blaming him for being here. If she wouldn't have gone on and on and *on* about how great a place the island was, he never would have come here to visit. How was he to know that he'd fall in love with the place, too? So, really, it was *her* fault he was here.

There, now he felt a tad less guilty about that look she'd given him. The one that had claimed Belle Island as her own—*not* his.

"What do you say, Coop? I'm thinking we should head back. I gotta get to work."

Cooper stood, stretched in a bow, then looked at him, his bright blue eyes eager and ready to go. He swore Cooper understood every word he said.

"Let's go."

They headed off down the beach, walking at the water's edge. Suddenly his quiet, simple life here on the island wasn't quite as simple as it had been.

CHAPTER 8

"Robin, do you know a Noah McNeil?" Sara questioned Robin as soon as she found her in the office at the inn.

"Noah? Sure. He runs the community center. He also volunteers at a ton of community events. Last I heard, he updated the town website, too. Why?" Robin narrowed her eyes.

"Oh, no reason. I just ran into him on the beach this morning."

"Ah, out with Cooper, I bet."

"You know his dog, too?"

"Everyone knows Cooper. He's… friendly." She laughed. "And Noah brings him to the community center quite often. Why the interest in him?"

She wasn't about to tell the whole sorry tale about how she'd gotten dumped without a word, even if Robin was one of her best friends. Some things were better left unsaid. "No interest, just wondering."

Robin sent her a look that said she didn't quite believe her.

"So, did the ordering get sorted out?" She changed the subject.

"Yes, I have everything ordered that Jay said we needed, but we're going to have to pay for them, and with Lil headed for rehab—"

Her cell phone dinged. Another text from Diane. "I've got to get this. My boss. But, anyway, I'm going to go by the hospital this afternoon. Aunt Lil talked to her banker and got new signature cards for me to sign so I can write checks while she's away."

"Good plan."

"I also told her we're going to get her signed up for online banking. She didn't object, just said she hadn't had time to figure it out and do it herself."

"She's a sharp lady. I'm sure she'll pick it up in no time and wonder how she did without it."

"I'm sure she will." She hoped so, anyway. "If you've got this paperwork under control, I'm going to go answer my boss's text and then help wait tables."

"Good plan. Oh, and I took out a want ad on the town website saying we were looking for workers. Jay says we need like two more. A server and help with cleaning the cottages."

"I've never hired anyone…"

"I have. Jay and I can do the interviews if you like."

"That would be perfect." But guilt crept over her with all the work her friends were doing for her. "Thanks, Robin. Really. I couldn't do this without you."

"That's what best friends are for."

When Robin walked into the kitchen that afternoon, Jay had managed to fix the dishwasher and was running dishes through it. He was standing with a fan blowing near him, his ever-present t-shirt stretched tight across his chest. *I like coffee, my dog, and maybe two people.*

"Nice shirt." She walked up to him and looked at the piled-up dishes. "Maybe I should have put an ad in for a dishwasher person too."

"Wouldn't be a bad idea. Or someone to

help clear tables *and* run the dishes. The dining room seems to get busier every year. And this weekend is the official opening of the summer tourist season with the Beach Blast Festival Noah started a few years back."

She frowned again. "Sara was asking about Noah."

"She knows him?" Jay lounged against the counter.

"She ran into him on the beach this morning and was just asking about him." She shook her head against the thought that Sara hadn't quite told her everything. "Anyway, I hope you don't mind. I told Sara that you and I would do the interviews."

"Don't mind at all. Anything to help out Lil. She took a chance on me giving me this job. I'd do anything for her."

"You're such an improvement over her last cook. I'm sure she'll never let you leave." She grinned at him.

He tossed her a lazy smile in return. "Well, good thing I have no plans to go, then."

He pushed off the counter and grabbed a towel and started a methodical wiping off of the counters. Spray. Wipe. Spray. Wipe. She watched as his strong hands scrubbed down the surface.

He turned to look at her. "So, I heard Marvin's Sporting Goods is being sold. You going to be out of a job soon?"

"Looks that way. Probably by next week." She stared down at her feet, debating whether to go on or not. But Jay always had a sympathetic ear. She looked at him and sighed. "*And...* I just heard that the owner of the cottage I'm renting has sold the place. I was on a month-to-month lease, so I'm out of there by the end of the month. So, now I need to find a new place to live *and* a job."

"Timing could be better, huh?"

"I'll say. But, whatever. I'll figure it out. Surely all my experience in accounting and running The Wishing Shop before this job at Marvin's will count for something."

"I've got a couch," he offered. "You know, until you find a place."

"I might have to take you up on that... though wouldn't the town gossips have a field day with that?"

"I don't much listen to town gossip." He grinned. "Well, I *listen* to it, I just don't put much stock in it."

"Thanks for the offer, but I'll figure something out."

"The offer stands."

"Thanks, Jay."

She turned and walked out of the kitchen, suddenly over-warm. Maybe they should look into getting a bit more cooling for the kitchen…

Jay watched Robin leave the kitchen, her hair swirling at her shoulders, her steps quick and determined. She'd had a couple of jobs around town since he'd been here. Managing a gift shop and the accounting department at Marvin's. She didn't look particularly upset with all the upheaval in her life.

But then, maybe Robin was hiding it from everyone, especially Sara since she was having such a rough time now and didn't want to burden her.

Though, didn't women friends talk about every little detail going on in their lives? Women, they were a strange bunch, and he'd never understand them.

He shrugged and went back to cleaning the

kitchen. That was one thing he needed when he cooked. A spotless kitchen to work in. And cooking and kitchens were things he *did* understand.

CHAPTER 9

Sara was pleased to see Aunt Lil sitting up,
her hair done, and a tray of food—mostly
eaten—beside her bed.

"You're looking better." She crossed over
and kissed her aunt.

"Feeling a bit better."

She turned at the sound of someone
entering the room.

"Oh, Dr. Harden, this is my niece, Sara."

A young woman in a white coat came over
to the bedside. "Nice to meet you."

"Dr. Harden here is a special friend of
Willie's. Do you remember him? He owns The
Lucky Duck on Oak Street."

"I remember him." She did, sort of.

"I'm going to send your aunt to rehab

tomorrow. I've got her all set up at a very good one over on the mainland."

"I still think I'd be fine at home," Aunt Lil insisted.

"You need physical therapy and a chance to get stronger. I promise we'll get you back home as soon as possible." Dr. Harden smiled encouragingly at Aunt Lil as if she understood how hard this was on her.

"I'll come visit as much as I can, Aunt Lil."

"But there's the Beach Blast this weekend. We have a booth there, you know."

No, she hadn't known. She wondered if all the plans for that had already been finalized. She'd have to check into that when she got back to the diner.

"It's good publicity for the inn and our expanded dining room."

"I've got everything under control. Don't worry." Just another tiny stretch of the truth.

"But I'm not sure how long you can stay. I know you're very busy with your own job."

"I'll stay as long as I'm needed. I'm doing some work remotely." As if to prove her point, her phone dinged. She glanced at it and slipped it away. Another text from Diane. The woman must text her a hundred times a day. At least. As it was, she was working long hours at the inn and most nights on the presentation for Diane.

"Lil will be taken good care of at the rehab center. And I'll pop over there to check on her, too," Dr. Harden assured her.

"See, everything will be just fine." She hoped it would be fine and she wasn't doing yet another one of her numerous stretches of the truth.

Robin sat with Charlotte and Sara on the chairs lining the private deck at The Nest watching the sunset once again. Sara looked exhausted. Robin hadn't missed that Sara's phone had dinged almost non-stop with texts from her boss. Between her friend trying to answer her boss, visit Lil, and work at the inn... it was no surprise she was so tired.

Robin poured them all glasses of wine as they settled into their chairs. "Long day, huh?"

"It was." Sara stretched out her legs.

"I thought I was used to standing for hours because I stand when I paint, but I admit to being very glad to be off my feet now." Charlotte kicked off her shoes.

"I really appreciate all the help you guys are giving me." Sara turned to look at Robin. "But how about your job? Your real job? Are you taking vacation to do this?"

She didn't want to worry Sara but didn't want to lie to her either. She let out a long sigh. "My job is ending. Marvin sold the sporting goods shop. There are just a few hours of work left there for me. I only agreed to stay on to the end because Marvin was in a bit of a panic when news got out he sold the business and most of the employees found new jobs."

"You're out of work? You should let me pay you for helping me at the inn."

"Nope. Not going to happen. I'm glad to help."

"But I—"

"Don't argue with me. You know you won't win, anyway."

Sara smiled. "Probably not. But I wish you'd let me."

"So you know that the inn does a booth at the festival this weekend, right?" She changed the subject from her job—or lack thereof.

"So I heard. Do you know if anything is planned for it?" Sara grimaced.

"Jay said most of it is all ready to go. Lil

usually closes the dining room here and just runs the booth on the festival weekend. Jay's got the food planned for the booth and has two workers coming to help him."

"Oh, you mean we get the weekend off?" Charlotte rubbed her foot. "I could get into a weekend off."

"Char, it's only been a couple days." She shook her head.

"I'm not used to painting walls. My shoulders and my feet ache."

"You don't have to," Sara insisted.

"Yes, I do. You need help. And it keeps me busy so I don't just sit and fret about my... I don't know what to call it. Lack of creativity? Painter's block?"

"I thought things were going great with your painting." Robin leaned forward so she could see Charlotte's face when she answered. She'd always been able to read Charlotte's face like a book.

"It is. Well, it was. But then... I didn't get the last gallery show I wanted. The remarks were that my work wasn't fresh or new." Charlotte sighed. "And I get that. I haven't felt much inspiration with my work lately. More like I'm just painting because it's what I do."

71

"You should set up a place to paint while you're here. There's the sunroom here on the wing. It has its own outside entrance. You can come and go as you please," Sara offered. "There are glass French doors closing it off from the rest of The Nest. Use it. Maybe being someplace new will inspire you."

"Maybe. But I'm going to be busy working on the furniture." Charlotte looked doubtful.

"Go out and get an easel and paints. Seriously. Take this time to just play with your painting and see what happens." Sara reached out and took Charlotte's hand. "Sometimes when I'm stuck on coming up with a creative idea for a client I go out and do something totally different. Once I came up with the best idea when I went to a park near where I work and just walked around instead of sitting at my desk, staring at the computer, and coming up with nothing. Please. Just try it."

"I might..."

"Good, that's settled. Charlotte for sure will set up a studio in the sunroom." Robin grinned. "Don't you argue with me either."

"Wouldn't dream of it."

Robin settled back in her chair, perfectly content to be here with her friends. It had been so long and she didn't realize how much she'd missed them. Well, not perfectly content. She still had the problem of finding a job and a place to live… But that wasn't her friends' problem. It was hers, and hers alone. Besides, she'd never been good at accepting help.

CHAPTER 10

Sara looked around the crowds at the Beach Blast. Who knew this many people could crowd onto Oak Street and Main Street? A band was playing in the gazebo at the end of Oak Street and people mingled in and out of the shops. The streets were closed to car traffic and booths lined the middle of the streets.

She and Charlotte wandered down the street, sampling food and browsing the craft booths. "This is kind of fun, isn't it? I wonder how long they've been doing this festival." Sara picked up a pretty scarf and held it up to her neck.

"That looks good with your eyes." Charlotte nodded. "But I don't know about the festival. They didn't have it when we lived here. I think

Robin said that the guy who runs the community center started the festival, and they have it annually now."

"It's a great way to bring in the summer tourist season." Charlotte picked up a floppy straw hat. "What do you think?"

"It's you, Char."

"I think so, too." She bought the hat and plopped it on her coppery red hair.

It did look good on her, but then everything looked good on Charlotte. She was that woman. Everyday clothes, fancy clothes, heels, flats, makeup, no makeup. Didn't matter. Charlotte was beautiful but never seemed to realize it. She often wore a mix of bohemian style clothing that seemed to suit her free-spirited painter self.

Sara frowned. If her friend had a painter self now. She'd gone out and bought an easel, a canvas, and paints. But Sara had seen no sign of any painting going on.

They made their way to the end of the block where a three-legged race was starting. Sara was surprised to see that Noah was coordinating the race. "Okay, kids, grab your partners. My helpers will get you all three-legged up."

The kids laughed as their legs were cobbled together. Noah roamed through the throng, adjusting tie-ups here and there, encouraging the kids.

"Okay, make your way to the starting line." Noah motioned to a chalk line on the ground.

She was pretty sure her mouth dropped open. Noah McNeil running an event at a festival. A *kid's* event. As far as she knew, he didn't even *like* kids. Or at least he hadn't back when she knew him. They often commented how kids were like aliens to them. She pretty much still felt that way because she was never around them. She didn't run with a mommy crowd back in Boston and she had no siblings, so no nieces or nephews. Just a totally different life.

But, Noah? There he was looking all in his element helping a duo of young girls who fell and giving the eye to two boys who tried to get a bit of an early start.

"Okay. On your mark. Get set... go!" Noah called out.

The kids laughed and tumbled and hurried to the finish line.

"We have a winner." Noah held up the arms of two boys. "Bobby and Mikey."

"Told you'd we win." Bobby, the blonde-haired boy, pumped his fist.

Robin caught up to them. "There you are. I didn't think I'd ever find you in this crowd."

"The festival is a great addition to the town." Charlotte looked around at the milling crowd.

"Yep, some things change here, but most things stay the same." Robin shrugged and turned to wave to Noah. "Hey, Noah," she called out.

He lifted a hand in a wave.

No, don't come over here.

Robin motioned for him to come over. She glared at Robin, who remained oblivious to what she'd done. Her friend raised an eyebrow in question, but by then Noah was walking up to them, Cooper by his side.

"Wanted to introduce you to my friends. I guess you met Sara on the beach the other day."

Noah gave her a questioning look but just nodded at her.

"And this is my friend, Charlotte. We all grew up together here on the island, though the two of them ran away from home and left me here alone." Robin grinned.

Sara knew Robin had never wanted to live any place but Belle Island. She loved living there.

"Nice to meet you." Noah smiled at Charlotte but still didn't give away their secret, for which she was thankful.

"Noah runs the community center and did most of the planning for the festival." Robin went on, oblivious to the war waging through Sara. "Noah's a great guy and we're glad he moved to the island. Always love another person we can talk into volunteering for stuff." Robin laughed.

Sara scowled.

She didn't want to hear what a great guy Noah was. Because he *wasn't* a great guy. He'd left her. Left her without a word. Just because she'd gotten the promotion they'd both worked for. A person who did that was *not* a nice guy.

Robin gave her a strange look.

"I should go." Sara broke up the let's-praise-Noah-fest. "I'm going to check on the inn's booth and see if Jay needs any help."

"Oh, I was just there talking to him. He's doing fine. Has his workers with him. Everything's going smoothly."

Now, what was she going to use as an excuse to escape?

"Mr. McNeil?" The blonde-haired boy who won the race came up to Noah.

"What do you need, Bobby?"

"Can I take Cooper for a walk?"

"Tell you what. How about we both take him for a walk? Let's go check with your mom first."

"She's right over there." He pointed to the gazebo.

"If you'll excuse me. I think Cooper here is getting a walk."

She watched while Noah, Cooper, and the boy walked away, getting lost in the crowd. She couldn't get over this Noah. The one who was comfortable around kids... even good with them.

Robin turned and stared at her. "What was that all about?"

"What?"

"The friction. The looks. What are you hiding?"

"I'm not *hiding* anything." She looked at where Noah had disappeared into the crowd. "I just... well, I used to know him."

"You did? When?"

"Years ago. Used to work together at the same ad agency."

"Huh. That's quite a coincidence." Charlotte stared at her, too.

"Really, that's it." She shrugged her shoulders to punctuate her point.

"And yet you didn't say a word when you asked me about him."

"I was just surprised, that's all."

"If you say so." Robin eyed her skeptically.

Charlotte wandered off to look at the painting competition, and Robin said she had to run. Sara wandered around the festival on her own, feeling strangely out of place in the town she'd grown up in. So much had changed. She ran into some people she knew and chatted with them, but mostly it was tourists milling about. Or maybe they were townspeople and she just didn't recognize them as such since she'd been gone so long...

She stopped by the inn's booth. "Hey, Jay. How's it going?"

"Going great. I just got back from the inn with more food for the booth. Doing a brisk business, but luckily I planned for it."

"Have you seen Robin?"

"Oh, she went to go look at a rental place. Apartment, I think."

She frowned. "I thought she lived in a cottage by the bay."

"She did, but the owner sold it. She's got to move by the end of the month." Jay turned away to wait on a customer.

Robin hadn't said a word to her. Not a word. So she was out of a job *and* a place to live. Well, that wasn't going to happen. She pulled out her phone and texted Charlotte and Robin.

Come to the inn when you're finished. I'm grabbing sandwiches for us from the booth. See you soon.

CHAPTER 11

C harlotte wandered around the display of local artwork. She looked at the painting that won first place in the art show. A painting of a young girl sitting on the beach. Peaceful. Serene. Just an everyday scene. The painting tugged at her. So simple, so moving, as if the artist had poured her heart into the painting.

She wanted that again. To pour her heart into her art. Her own paintings didn't move her anymore. She didn't know what had changed, but something had. Her splashes of color and impressionistic style just... well, it wasn't talking to her anymore. It had been the trend, and she'd ridden it well. But now that trend was sinking, along with her career.

Painter's block. That's what she had. Like writer's block for painters. Did writer's block last this long? Like for over a year long...

She felt like a fraud now. Not a real painter. Really, a painter who hadn't painted a decent new piece of work in over a year? Maybe she was all finished. Painted out all her creativity. Nothing remarkable left in her.

At least she had the furniture to work on for the cottages now. She'd had such fun picking out the furniture and the colors for the walls. Even if her shoulders still ached from all the wall painting. But the teal cottage had turned out nicely if she did say so herself. A pale teal on the walls and crisp white on the trim.

She'd also picked out darker shades of teal chalk paint for the furniture. At least she had that much creativity left in her. She couldn't wait to get started on them tomorrow. She could picture the perfect coastal decor for the cottage and enjoyed helping Sara out with it.

Her phone dinged, and she slipped it from her pocket. A text from Sara.

She took one last look at the paintings and turned to head back to the inn.

Sara set out the sandwiches on the dining table in the small kitchen in The Nest. Then she pulled out some wine glasses and raided Aunt Lil's red wine stash for another bottle. This time she planned on winning an argument with Robin. And Charlotte for that matter. They'd both been unbelievably helpful with the inn. She was going to repay them for their kindness.

"Hey, there." Charlotte came walking in the back door with Robin close behind her.

"What's with the mysterious text?" Robin looked at the table. "And a sit-down meal?"

"Yes, sit. We need to talk."

Charlotte and Robin slipped into their chairs and she poured them all a glass of wine. She took a sip of hers as she sat across from them and squared her shoulders. "So, this is how it's going to work…"

Robin raised an eyebrow.

"Robin, you're going to move into the yellow cottage."

"What—no—"

"Yes. I know it's not finished now, but it's all I have to offer. The rooms are mostly filled up at the inn. I know you're out of a place to stay by the end of the month. Charlotte, if you don't mind moving into the cottage, too? It has two bedrooms so you'll both have your own space."

"I can't just move in there." Robin shook her head.

"Why not? Did you find another place to live and a job today?" Sara pinned Robin with what she hoped was a definitive stare.

"No, but—"

"So, it's decided. You'll move in. The yellow cottage isn't rented out yet. Jay said Aunt Lil wasn't sure they could get both cottages finished, so they just put the teal cottage on the books for rental. So, if you don't mind living in a cottage while it's being remodeled…"

"I couldn't just live there…"

"Of course, you could." Charlotte chimed in. "You're always the one to jump in and help other people. Learn to accept some help yourself."

"Besides, then you're right here to help me with the inn." Sara grinned. "See, it's just to help me out, really."

Robin frowned. "I don't know…"

"Robin, this is one argument you're not going to win. Please let me do this for you. You've been so helpful." Sara turned to

Charlotte. "*Both* of you have been so helpful. Please let me do this for you."

Robin let out a long sigh. "Well... I will under one condition."

"What's that?" She eyed Robin.

"You tell us what's going on between you and Noah." Robin pinned her with a stare.

"Yes, what *is* going on between you two?" Charlotte asked.

"Nothing is going on between us."

"What *did* go on between you? In the past." Robin was not going to let it go.

She sighed. "Okay, so we dated. For almost a year. I thought things were kind of serious."

"When was this?" Charlotte leaned forward in her chair, encouraging her to keep talking.

"Years ago. Over twenty years. It's silly this is even coming up again."

"And yet, it's part of our deal. You talk, I move into the cottage."

She closed her eyes against the memories swirling around, then opened them and continued. "We were working at the same ad agency. Dated. Helped each other out on our projects. We just... clicked... you know?"

Sara reached for her wine and took a sip,

thinking back on how she'd been totally smitten with Noah. She'd just about decided she loved him. Ha, look how that turned out. "But then we were both up for the same promotion. Whoever got the promotion was going to be the boss of the other. I got the promotion. Noah disappeared that very same day. Left his job with no notice. Never said a word to me."

Robin frowned. "That doesn't sound like the Noah I know."

"It didn't sound like the one I thought I knew either. I guess he couldn't stand the idea that I'd be his boss. Honestly, we both thought that he'd get the promotion. He had an edge on me, I was sure of it. And he'd worked there a bit longer. But I got the promotion and, *poof,* he was gone from my life."

"Well, that's not cool." Charlotte scowled. "We don't like people who treat our Sara like that. Robin, maybe you should change your opinion of Noah."

Robin looked thoughtful. "Maybe. But it sure doesn't sound like the Noah I know."

"Now can we change the subject?" Sara leaned back in her chair. "I did what you asked. I told you about Noah, so Robin, you're moving to the cottage. Now eat your supper and then let's bring our wine out onto the deck."

"Yes, ma'am." Robin grinned at her.

For once in her life, Sara had won an argument with Robin… kind of.

CHAPTER 12

The next morning Sara hurried to the market for flour. They hadn't quite gotten their ordering of supplies down and Jay needed more flour for pies. She could do that. Charlotte was busy painting the furniture for the teal cottage, and Robin was moving some of her things into the yellow cottage and arranging for storage of the furniture she had in her old rental. She still insisted she'd find a new place as soon as possible. But Sara had just rolled her eyes and said there was no hurry to move out. Besides, she liked having her friends so close.

She bought the flour, stashed it in two large carrying bags, and headed back out to the sunny street. She had walked to the market but was kind of regretting that decision now. She paused to adjust the flour in the grocery totes.

As she balanced the bags in her hands, she glanced across the street. There, across the road and a few doors down, was Noah. She ducked into the doorway of a shop, not wanting to be seen. But she probably hadn't needed to do that. He only had eyes for the young woman who'd rushed up to him and thrown her arms around his neck. She could hear his delighted laugh drift across in the breeze as he swung her around. He kissed her cheek and hugged her.

The woman was cute and beautiful in that adorable, bubbly way some young women had. That was just great. Now he was dating younger women. She looked to be about half his age at most. Well, fine. It didn't matter one bit to her.

The young woman's laughter joined Noah's as she pulled out of the embrace.

Sara walked out of the doorway and headed down the sidewalk, deliberately not turning around to take another look... until she did. It was hard to miss the overjoyed and adoring look on Noah's face.

A flash of jealousy rushed through her. Which was crazy, of course. There was nothing to be jealous of.

And she despised the man, anyway.

So it made no difference to her who he dated. Who made him laugh. Who made him light up with elation.

No difference at all.

She sucked in a deep breath, chasing away the memories that threatened to escape from the tightly walled off box in her mind, and hurried down the sidewalk, no longer noticing the weight she carried, just wanting to escape all things Noah.

"Thanks, Jay." Robin straightened and looked at the bed Jay had helped her set up in her bedroom in the yellow cottage. "I appreciate the help."

"It was nice of Sara to offer to let you stay here."

Robin rolled her eyes. "It didn't escape me that you were probably the one who told her I was out of a place to stay."

"Me?" His innocent look didn't fool her. "And hey, I offered up my place for you to stay."

"Right." She rolled her eyes again.

"Let's get Charlotte's bed set up, then I'm

back to the kitchen. Sara went to get me more flour. I forgot to add that to your list. Going to make pies for dinner tonight."

"Um, I love your pies." She forgot she was exasperated at him for telling Sara about her troubles.

"Good, then come have a slice tonight and say you forgive me." He threw her an impish smile.

The man was impossible. She hid a grin and headed into Charlotte's bedroom. They put the frame together and wrestled the queen mattress onto the bed. She flopped down on it. "That was more work than I thought it would be."

Jay plopped down on the mattress beside her, looking at the walls. "We probably should have painted the walls first before you guys moved in, but really, we needed the room that Charlotte's been staying in at the inn. We're almost full through the entire summer."

"Well, that's good."

"Good and bad. Good income, but a lot of work. I'm sure Lil is stressing about not being here."

"Sara said Lil is already making noise about leaving the rehab place and coming back to the inn. Luckily her doctor was still able to cut her off and convince her to stay a bit longer."

"She should be concentrating on getting stronger." Jay propped himself up on his elbows.

"Hopefully she will. And maybe we'll have everything finished by the time she gets home. Anyway, we'll just shove the beds into the middle of the rooms when we paint the walls." She rolled over and crawled off the bed. "I better start unloading my car. It's full of clothes and stuff."

"Need help?" Jay sat up.

"No, I'll let you get back to your pies."

"I'll see you later for that piece of pie."

She walked him to the door and watched as he headed down the pathway back to the inn, the sunshine glinting off his sandy blonde hair. He was a helpful one, that Jay Turner.

CHAPTER 13

"Robin? You here?" Sara walked into the yellow cottage.

"Back here trying to conquer my clothes."

Sara made her way to the back bedroom and found Robin sitting on the bed, surrounded by clothes in stacks and on hangers.

"Wow, you've got some unpacking to do."

"Well, it's unpacked, it's just not put away or hung up."

Sara grabbed an armload of hanging clothes and went to the closet, settling them on the clothes rod. "There."

"I realized after I dumped these stacks of clothes out of boxes that I don't have a dresser."

"Right. Charlotte bought a couple for here, but she hasn't painted them yet. We can look in the storeroom and see if there are any old dressers in there you and Char can use until she finishes the ones for the cottage."

"Probably a good idea. Otherwise, I need to pack all this back up and riffle through boxes every time I get dressed." Robin climbed off the bed.

They headed off to the inn and slipped into the storage room. The room was much smaller now since Aunt Lil had taken most of it to enlarge the dining room. They did find a dresser and a chest of drawers in the corner. A little beat up, but serviceable. "Charlotte will probably want to paint these after she finishes up what she has." Sara pushed on the dresser as Robin tugged on it. "She's painting everything she can get her hands on."

"She has to let me use it first." Robin paused. "We need a dolly or something to move these."

Jay walked into the room. "I thought I heard a commotion in here."

"We're taking a dresser and that chest of drawers." Sara pointed. "Robin and Char need them at the cottage."

"I'll get them, put them in the van, and bring them over as soon as I'm finished with the pies. Oh, and there's an extra small table and chairs in that little storage area upstairs. Lil thought it was too wobbly, but I fixed it. I'll bring that over, too."

"Thanks, Jay." Sara was more than willing to let him wrestle the furniture.

She and Robin left the storeroom with Jay trailing behind them.

"You coming for that piece of pie?" Jay paused when they got to the back door and looked at Robin.

"Maybe later. Got a lot of work to do." Robin ducked her head, almost sprinting out the door, and started down the pathway back to the cottage.

"What kind of pie?" Sara eyed Jay.

"Peach pie and pecan pie."

"I'll be over later for some. I swear you're like some kind of miracle worker for Aunt Lil. Best cook she's ever had, *and* you know how to fix things."

"And I deliver furniture." He grinned.

"That, too." She headed out the door and hurried to catch up with Robin. "Hey, what's your hurry?"

"Just a lot to do."

It seemed more like she was avoiding Jay,

but maybe not. Sara hadn't quite figured out what was going on between him and Robin. Friends? More than friends? Less than friends?

They reached the cottage and Robin sank onto a brightly painted chair on the front porch. "It's humid today, isn't it?" She waved her hand in front of her face.

Sara sat beside her. "It is."

"Let me get us some ice water." Robin jumped up and soon came back with two big glasses. "At least the fridge still works. And there is a coffee pot. I need my coffee."

"I hear you on that." Sara reached for a glass and took a long swallow of the cool liquid.

They sat in silence for a bit, watching as people walked out of the inn and along the pathways between the cottages, most of them headed for the beach.

Sara finally couldn't help herself and turned to Robin, a bit exasperated at herself that she was going to ask the question. "So do you know who Noah's girlfriend is?"

Robin frowned. "Girlfriend? I don't think he's dating anyone now. Not that I've heard of. Why?"

"I saw him in town. He was with a younger woman. He was obviously thrilled to see her."

She hated the flash of jealousy that swept through her, so she resolutely ignored it. Really, she did. "The woman threw herself into his arms, so there has to be something going on."

Robin frowned, then smiled. "Did she have long chestnut brown hair? And was she really short?"

"Yes, that's the one." It sounded like her anyway.

Robin laughed. "That's his niece, Zoe. She must be back in town."

She tried to think back on what she knew about Noah's family. He had one sister. She vaguely remembered something about him becoming an uncle. Or maybe he'd already become one when she met him? She wasn't sure, because really, all they usually did was work or talk about projects or clients. Rarely about family. "His niece? Well, that's nice that she's close to him and came to visit him."

"Of course she's close to him. He raised her."

She set her glass down with a clatter on the table between them. "He what?"

"I don't know the full story. I just know when he came to town, he brought Zoe with him. I heard his sister and her husband died.

101

Not sure how. Just that he'd been raising Zoe for some time before he came here. Zoe took to the town just like Noah did. Loved it here. Then she went off to college, then just took a job somewhere. I think maybe up by Orlando. Noah seems a bit lost without her here with him. Quite an adjustment, I'm sure."

"He *raised* her?" Sara could not get her mind to wrap around that thought.

"Yes, and he did a great job. She's a wonderful young woman. Sharp, funny, and just as giving as Noah."

Noah? Giving? And raising a child? It just wasn't meshing with the Noah she knew. Or thought she'd known.

She took another sip of ice water and looked out at the palm fronds blowing in the slight breeze. Her phone beeped, and she flipped it over on the table. She didn't feel like being at Diane's beck and call right now.

Robin looked at her curiously. "You okay?"

"You know what? I'm not sure… Everything is kind of topsy-turvy right now."

"Who says topsy-turvy these days?" Robin raised an eyebrow.

"Me. When my life is like this."

"Zoe, you're back in town." Tally gave Zoe a hug as she and Noah entered Magic Cafe.

"Just a quick day trip. Rumor has it Uncle Noah misses me."

"I do." He smiled at Zoe.

"Come on. I'll seat you with a front-row view of the gulf."

They followed Tally and took their seats. Zoe looked out at the water. "Wow, I miss this. I was used to just walking a couple of blocks over to the beach. Orlando is just so… landlocked." She tossed back her head laughed. He'd missed her laugh.

He wanted to say she could just move back home but held his tongue. Wasn't it a parent's job to raise their children so they were independent? Not that he was really a parent, and Zoe wasn't his child. But he felt like a parent and she felt like his child. What an unexpected blessing she'd been. Even if he'd been scared witless when he'd heard his sister and brother-in-law had died and he had custody of Zoe. He couldn't believe anyone in their right mind would give him a child to raise.

Of course, he'd agreed to be her guardian

when they'd asked him right after she was born. But whoever really thinks they'll actually become the guardian?

They ordered sweet tea and grouper sandwiches. And he settled back in his chair, so happy for this time with his niece.

"You getting along okay?" She looked closely at him.

"Don't worry about me. I'm fine."

"I do worry about you."

He could see the concern in her eyes, so he changed the subject. "How's the new job coming along?"

"Oh, I love it. There's a group of us new to the company. Been hanging out a bit with them after work. Joined a gym since I don't have the beach to jog on."

He was so happy to hear it was working out well for her.

"You know, there are a lot of huge community centers and activity centers in all the retirement communities near me. You could always apply to one of those..." She looked at him.

He laughed. "I'm fine, really." Though it would be nice to be closer to her... But, really, she needed her space, right?

"You could at least look into them. I hear they pay pretty well." She smiled at Tereza, the waitress who delivered their tea. "Hey, Tereza."

"Hi, Zoe. Glad to see you back in town."

"I thought I should come back and check up on Uncle Noah."

"You do not have to check up on me. I'm fine." He reached for his glass and took a swallow of the cool, slightly sweet tea. Magic Cafe had the best sweet tea. Well, so did Charming Inn, but he wasn't going to chance running into Sara again. Especially not with Zoe. Zoe was a sharp one and might catch on to the undercurrent that seemed to flow around Sara and him.

"He practically single-handedly organized and ran the Beach Blast Festival." Tereza waved to someone who just sat down and turned back to them. "We had a great turnout."

"See? I'm so busy these days I hardly notice you're gone." Which was a big, fat lie.

Zoe shook her head. "Right. Don't believe you for a moment. You miss me walking with you on the beach. You miss my cooking. You miss watching scary movies with me."

"Okay, yes, I miss that. But really, Zoe, I'm fine."

"Your food should be up soon." Tereza walked away to wait on another table.

"Are you sure you're okay?" Zoe asked once again.

He didn't know what he could say to reassure her. And he was the adult. He should be reassuring *her* and worrying about *her*.

"I know you love Belle Island, but you should maybe look into those jobs up near Orlando. It would be great to have you near again."

He did love living on Belle Island, but he loved Zoe more. Maybe he would look into some of those positions up near where she lived now. Maybe this was her way of saying she needed him closer by. Yes, he'd put out some feelers about those jobs. Though he would hate to leave the island.

But he'd do anything that Zoe needed. Anything.

CHAPTER 14

Monday, Noah took Cooper for their normal morning walk. Only this time they walked in the opposite direction of the lighthouse. No use taking a chance of running into Sara again, since he knew she loved that lighthouse. She'd always talked about how special it was, and he'd agree with her. There was something extraordinary about it.

They headed down the beach with Cooper doing his chase the birds and trot back to walk beside him routine. Then Cooper raced down the beach toward a lone woman walking their direction. It didn't escape him that the woman looked just like Sara. With flowing brown hair and— yep, he was sure it was her. Coop, the traitor, ran circles around her, his tail wagging.

She leaned down to pet Coop, then looked up the beach toward him.

No way to escape her now. Not without leaving Coop. He jogged down the beach toward them.

"Morning," he said as he reached her.

"Morning." She looked surprised to see him.

For a brief moment, he wondered if she'd walked this way on the beach to avoid seeing him, too. How had that worked out for both of them?

Sara petted Coop again, then looked up at him. "So your niece was in town yesterday?"

He looked at her in surprise now. "How—" Well, of course most of the locals would know Zoe had been in town. News traveled quickly on Belle Island. "Yes, just for the day."

"That's nice."

"It was."

They stood there looking at each other. His niece, the elephant in the room, so to speak. The reason everything had blown up between him and Sara. But he didn't regret his decision. Not one bit. Zoe meant everything to him.

He crossed his arms and stood silently.

Sara stood staring at Noah, noticing a bit of a beard growing on his face and his eyes looking… what? Protective?

She wanted to ask him about Zoe but didn't. Didn't really want to know what his life had been like since he left her. Didn't want to know what his life was like now. Just didn't want to know anything about him.

And yet… A small sigh escaped her. She exasperated herself yet again when she blurted out her question. "So, when did you start raising Zoe? Robin said your sister died but didn't know any details."

His mouth dropped open and he stared at her. His eyes narrowed. "What do you mean when did I get custody of Zoe?"

She frowned. It wasn't that hard of a question, was it? "How old was she? How long have you been raising her?"

"Cut it out." His voice was cold and sent icy shivers through her.

"What do you mean, cut it out?" Confusion and annoyance surged through her. It was one simple question. Why was he acting so strange?

"You know when I got custody. The same day I turned down that promotion at the ad agency."

"What do you mean you turned it down? *I* got the promotion."

"Right, after I turned it down. Because I couldn't take it. I'd just heard about my sister and brother-in-law. I had to leave."

"You left to take care of Zoe?" Nothing made sense. If he left to take care of her, why hadn't he just told her?

"I left you a note that I gave to Diane *and* I left you voice mail on your landline. Told you what happened. I knew you weren't a kid person, and Zoe was my responsibility, not yours. I told you to call if you still wanted to date, but it would have to be long-distance." He shrugged. "You never called, so I realized that my taking on Zoe wasn't part of your plans for climbing the corporate ladder."

"I didn't get any note *or* a message."

He looked at her long and hard. "You didn't? I called a couple days after I left—maybe a week—it was all a blur. I looked for you for a few minutes that day but couldn't find you, and I had to get to Zoe. So I left a note with Diane."

"Diane didn't give it to me and didn't say a word."

"I just jotted it on a piece of paper. Said I'd turned down the job and would call you and explain. I told her why I was leaving. Maybe she thought it wasn't her place to tell you, and that I'd tell you?" He frowned. "Or even more likely she didn't want you to know you were their second choice. Anyway, I did leave you a note. I had to get Zoe settled down. She was devastated and couldn't understand where her parents were. That's all I thought about for the first weeks."

She frowned. "No, I didn't get the note or the message. I thought you left because I got the promotion and you didn't want me to be your boss."

His reaction was maybe more surprised by that remark than when she asked about Zoe. "You thought I'd leave because *you* got the promotion over me getting it?"

"And yet, it appears you got it first."

"But you thought I was *that* kind of person? Who would leave over a *lost promotion?*" He stared at her hard once again. "I have no words, Sara. No words." He turned toward his dog. "Come on, Coop. Time to go."

"Noah, I—" Her heart pounded, and she reached out a hand.

"I guess I didn't really know you after all. You're not the person I thought you were if you'd think that about me. I thought you knew me. That we had something... special. I understood if you didn't want to be involved with me with all my newfound responsibilities with Zoe. I got that. But if you thought I was that shallow of a person to leave over not getting a promotion..." He shook his head. "Coop, come."

She watched him walk away, his shoulders set, and not turning around for even one glance back at her. She'd misjudged him. She should have known he wasn't the kind of guy to just disappear because she got the promotion. She'd had so much pride though, she hadn't been able to make herself call him.

But if she had called him back then, she would have known the truth.

Though, would knowing the truth have changed anything? What would she have decided about Noah with his new responsibility of raising Zoe?

And she didn't like herself very much when she thought she knew what she would have decided back then. She'd just been so very, very *focused*.

CHAPTER 15

Sara headed back to the inn and helped with the morning rush of diners, then went in search of Robin. She found her at the yellow cottage, painting the front room. "Here, let me help." She grabbed a paintbrush and the white paint can and began cutting in the trim. Not that she was very good at it.

After she'd gotten white paint on the freshly painted yellow walls three times, Robin took the brush out of her hands. "I'll get the trim."

She sighed. "I'm sorry. I guess painting trim isn't my strong suit."

Robin grinned. "I guess not."

Her phone dinged, and she glanced at it. Diane, of course.

"Why don't you go and work on your presentation for your boss? I've got this."

"I hate not helping."

"Trust me, you're helping me by *not* painting." Robin laughed.

She sank onto a chair and looked out the window for a moment. She should go work on her presentation, but she was just so out of sorts after running into Noah on the beach.

Robin glanced over at her and sank into the chair across from her. "What's up?"

Of course, Robin would pick up on her mood. She was like that. She could read almost anyone.

"I… I ran into Noah on the beach this morning."

"And?"

"And you were right about him and I was so… wrong."

Robin just sat and waited for her to go on.

"He didn't leave because I got the promotion. He actually got it and turned it down."

Robin frowned. "But why?"

"It happened right when he heard about his sister's death. He left to go take care of Zoe."

"So why didn't he tell you that?" Robin got

up and placed the roller in the paint tray and came back to sit down.

"He said he thought Diane would tell me and he left a note for her to give me. But she didn't. And he said he left me a message on my phone. My landline. Still had one back then." She looked at her cell phone. Life had been simpler in some ways with landlines. Like Diane wouldn't have been able to bug her a million times a day with constant texts and questions.

"But you didn't get it?"

"No…" She frowned and thought back on that crazy time when she'd gotten that first promotion and had been so hurt that Noah had left. She snapped her fingers. "Hey, remember when there was the fire in my apartment building?"

"I remember you telling me about that. It was a long time ago."

"It was about the time that Noah left. Our phones in the apartment building were messed up for weeks. Could he have left it then?"

"I guess. But why wouldn't he have tried to call you again? Or call you at work?"

"He said on the message he explained that he was going to raise Zoe and understood if I didn't want to be involved in all of that

115

responsibility. He said if he didn't hear from me he understood and he wished me the best."

"Now *that* sounds like the Noah I know." Robin pinned her with an I-told-you-so look.

"And this morning, he was hurt that I'd think he was the kind of person who'd leave over a job promotion. He said he thought we knew each other better than that." She sighed. "You were right about Noah. I was wrong. So very, *very* wrong. And I let my pride get in the way of doing what I should have done. I should have just picked up the phone and called him."

"So what are you going to do about it now?"

"Now? There's nothing I can do. It's water under the bridge. That ship has sailed. We lost our chance. We both have different lives now."

"Instead of spouting trite idioms at me, you could at least go find him and apologize. Make things right with him."

"I don't know... I don't think I can make it right."

"You could try." Robin pinned her with another of her famous listen-to-me gazes.

Sara pushed back from the table. "Okay, okay. I'll go talk to him." She grinned at Robin. "Better late than never."

Sara walked into the Belle Island Community center. A sign on a chalkboard proclaimed it was senior luncheon day in the main hall. She followed the signs until she came to a large open room. Tables were scattered around the room and a long buffet of sandwiches and desserts stretched along one wall. People were seated at the tables. Some playing cards, some just chatting, and a group of women sat knitting and laughing.

She saw Noah come walking in with two big pitchers of iced tea. He froze when he saw her, but then turned when someone asked him a question. He set the tea on the buffet and turned to leave.

She hurried up to him and caught his arm. "Noah. Can we talk?"

"What's the point, Sara?"

"The point is, I want to apologize."

He paused and looked directly into her eyes.

She took a big breath and blurted out all she'd been holding inside. "I was so hurt when you left. I realize now I jumped to the conclusion that you left because I got the promotion. But I couldn't figure out any other reason you'd just… leave like that. No goodbye, no word, nothing."

"But I did leave a message and a note."

"But I never got them. I think it must have been about the time when my apartment building had a fire. It was in a different wing than my apartment, I was lucky about that, but our phones were messed up for weeks."

He searched her face. "Come with me." He turned around and strode away. She hurried to catch up with him. He led her into a large office and motioned for her to sit down.

She sat on a chair across the desk from him. He sat down, then got back up and paced the floor, not saying a word. Then he turned and looked at her.

"I owe you an apology, too. I should have known if you got my message you would have called. If nothing more than to give your condolences about my sister. You'd never just drop out of my life when things were so… tough for me." He paced a few more steps. "I should have called you again. Or sent a letter or something." He shrugged. "I was just so overwhelmed with figuring out everything with Zoe. And, to be honest, I was hurt you didn't call me. I picked up the phone so many times to call you… but just never did. Besides, once I figured out how crazy my life was going to be raising Zoe, I was sure you'd want nothing of it. Not that I regret my decision. I adore Zoe. She's the best thing that ever happened to me, but it was super hard for both of us for a long time."

"I'm sorry I wasn't there for you. If I'd just called you… but my pride…" She stood and walked over to where he was standing by the window. "I'm sorry."

"We really messed it up, didn't we?"

She smiled at him. "We could have made better choices."

"We were prideful fools." He frowned. "So, let's make a better choice now. Would you go out with me?"

"Like on a date?"

He grinned. "Exactly like that. I pick you up. We go get something to eat. Honestly, I'd love to catch up with you. Hear what you've been up to."

"I'd like that, too." She would. She wanted to hear what he'd been doing with his life since he left… along with raising a child, of course. "You could come and eat at the inn tonight."

"Okay, it's a date."

"About seven? That way I can help with the first of the dinner crowd."

"Seven it is."

She started to leave but turned back to him. "And Noah, I'm sorry."

"I am, too." His voice was low and strong. "I'm very, *very* sorry."

Noah watched Sara walk away, and for the first time in a long time, his spirits soared. He'd missed her. Missed talking to her. Laughing with her at all hours when they pulled all-nighters working on some client presentation. They'd been good together. As friends, as coworkers, as a couple.

When he'd left that message all those years ago, he'd been certain she would call him. She would help him sort out the chaos of his life after his sister died. He'd checked his messages a dozen times a day for a week or more. Then he'd finally realized the call was never going to come.

If only he'd known that she never got the message and Diane hadn't given her his note. If only he'd called her again, instead of being too proud to call and ask her for help.

But *if only* didn't get a person anywhere in life. If only his sister and brother-in-law had taken a different route home that night, they wouldn't have been in the accident that had taken their lives.

But if his sister hadn't been killed, he'd never have had the enormous joy of raising Zoe. He'd probably still be the workaholic he'd been before, thinking kids were aliens and that work was the most important thing.

He walked over to the desk and picked up a photo of Zoe. "You're a good one, Zoe. You turned out great in spite of my too-many-to-count mistakes I made raising you." He set the photo down and walked back out to the main hall. He had seniors to check on and he'd promised to play a round of bridge with a group of the ladies.

CHAPTER 16

Robin walked into The Nest, with Charlotte right behind her. "So, what happened? Did you find Noah?"

Sara turned from where she was putting the dishes away. "I did."

"And?" Charlotte came over and lounged against the counter.

"And we're going on a date. Kind of. He's coming over to the inn and we're going to have dinner."

Robin scowled. "That's kind of a weak date, but okay. It's a start."

Was it a weak date? Was she getting it wrong already? "But I have to help Jay with at least the beginning of the dinner rush." She hoped justified the choice of where to go.

"I'll help him," Robin offered quickly.

"You've done enough. Like tons." She was so grateful for the help, but felt guilty for all her friends were doing for her.

"I'll help, too. Though I'm not much of a waitress, I can clear tables or help in the kitchen." Charlotte pushed off the counter. "And you're not wearing that, are you?"

She looked down at her khaki pants and teal blouse. "I... I hadn't really thought about it."

Charlotte took her by the shoulders and spun her around. "Come on. Let's go raid your closet."

Charlotte and Robin sat on the bed while she took out outfit after outfit. They shot down each one. "You either look like you're headed into a business meeting or flopping on a chair on the beach."

Her nervousness about tonight raised up a notch with every outfit they vetoed.

Robin jumped up. "I'll be right back. I have the perfect dress."

She came back in a few minutes with a simple sundress with flowers on it. "This. It will look great on you."

She tried it on and admitted it did look good.

"There. Now, I'm going to pull your hair back and twist it into a fancy knot. Sit."

She did as Charlotte ordered. After a touch of makeup, she stood in front of the mirror.

"See you look great." Robin nodded approvingly.

She snatched her cell off the dresser when it dinged. A text from Diane.

Don't forget I need that proposal from you by tomorrow at five. No later.

"Does your boss ever give you a moment's peace?" Charlotte shook her head.

"Not when we're in the middle of a big project. And not when I'm away from the office in the middle of it." She frowned. "Not that I've ever been away from the office when we're working on a presentation to snag a client like Coastal Furniture."

"You should take vacations sometimes." Charlotte took her phone away and put it back on the dresser.

She sighed. "I should. I really should. And

I'm going to come back here more often to check on Aunt Lil."

Robin looked skeptical.

"I am," she insisted.

"It would be great to see more of you." Robin sank onto the bed.

"I'm sure Lil will love that." Charlotte walked over to the dresser and picked up a pair of earrings. "Here, wear these, too."

She put on the earrings as commanded and twirled around in front of the full-length mirror. She liked this casual, beachy version of herself. "You two do a good job of dressing me." She smiled at her friends.

"Just part of the services we best friends offer." Robin popped back off the bed. "I should head to the dining room and see if Jay needs help."

"I feel terrible that you two are doing so much work."

"It's not a problem." Charlotte headed after Robin.

"Hey, wait for me. I'm going to help until Noah gets here." She hurried after them.

Noah glanced in the mirror. "What do you think, Coop? Do I look okay?"

Coop looked up from lounging on the floor and wagged his tail.

"I'll take that as a yes." Noah tucked his shirttail in, then untucked it. "That's better, right? A casual look?"

Coop didn't answer him this time.

He didn't know why he was so nervous. Yes, he did. He couldn't remember the last time he'd been on a date. He'd been so busy raising Zoe that he hadn't had time for dating. Zoe had tried to set him up a few times, but nothing had really come from it. He'd always grudgingly gone along with her fix-ups. He knew she just wanted him to be happy. But he'd become used to his bachelorhood. He was fine with it. Comfortable with it.

So why was he going out with Sara Wren of all people?

He reached down and ruffled the fur on Cooper's head. "I'll be back in a bit. Wish me luck."

Coop thumped his tail twice.

That meant good luck, Noah was sure of it.

He decided to walk to the inn. The heat of the day was abating with a nice evening breeze chasing away the humidity, and he was early, anyway.

He walked along the sidewalk, taking his time. He didn't want to show up so early that he looked over-eager. Though… he *was* kind of over-eager. He sucked in a deep breath of the salty air. He needed to get over himself. This was not a big deal. Not at all. Just a dinner with an old friend, playing catch up.

He stumbled on a crack in the sidewalk and caught himself. Since when could he not even walk down a sidewalk? He shook his head, watched his feet as he walked, and started counting his steps to keep his mind off this date.

He got to the inn only five minutes early. That was acceptable, right? He climbed the front stairs and walked inside. The air conditioning cooled him, and he took another deep breath as he walked across to the dining room.

He stood in the doorway and saw Sara busy talking to a table of customers. They laughed at something she said as she took their menus. The room was crowded for a weeknight, with only a few empty tables.

Robin walked up to him. "Hey, Noah. I saved you two a table near the window."

"Great." He followed her to the table and slipped into a chair.

"I'll go wrestle Sara away from her customers and send her over."

"If she's busy—"

"She's always busy. But tonight she's taking some time off to catch up with you. And I'm not taking no for an answer."

He didn't doubt that for a second. He'd learned long ago that no one argued with Robin.

CHAPTER 17

Sara turned around when Robin touched her arm. "Noah's here."

She looked over in the direction where Robin nodded. "I don't know. We're so busy tonight."

Robin took the menus from her hands. "And I'm taking over for you. Charlotte's helping in the kitchen."

"I can't leave you two working and go and just have dinner."

"Quit stalling. Go have dinner. You're allowed to take a break sometimes, you know."

"But—"

Robin glared at her. "Don't make me drag you over there. You're just nervous. Go." She gave her a little push.

Sara pasted on a smile and walked over to where Noah was waiting. He stood as she approached the table and held out the chair for her. Noah, always the gentleman. She remembered that much about him. She remembered a multitude of things about him, she just didn't let herself actually *think* about those memories.

He took his seat across from her. "I was afraid you weren't going to be able to get away."

"Robin didn't give me much choice. I've learned to never argue with her. I never win."

Noah's eyes sparkled. "She's rather persuasive."

She ducked her head to look at the menu instead of his eyes, which was ridiculous because she knew everything on it. But she stared at it, anyway.

Noah set his menu on the table. "Have you decided?"

"I think I'll have the red snapper."

"That's what I decided on, too."

They ordered their meals and some wine and sat sipping their drinks.

"It's getting warmer and warmer these days." Noah fiddled with the silverware beside his plate.

"Pretty soon it will be those oppressively hot and humid days where all you want to do is hang out on the beach." She leaned back in her chair and stretched her legs. They bumped against Noah's and she jerked them back and tucked them under her chair.

"How much longer do you think you'll be here?" He said it without any sign or reaction to her legs brushing his.

"I'm not sure. I want to get Aunt Lil settled back here. I should probably do a quick trip back home though. At least for a few days. Diane is breathing down my neck on a presentation."

"You still working for Diane?" He raised an eyebrow.

"Yes, but I'm up for a promotion. Partner. Then we'd be equals. Well, kinda. Not sure anyone is ever an equal to Diane."

"Good for you. I know that's what you always wanted."

"It was. Is. I mean... I do want the promotion, but there's some stiff competition. There's the guy that came on board after you left. Terrence. He acts like he's all helpful, but I get the feeling he's cutthroat behind my back. He's probably my biggest competition right now.

And, as a bonus, he's still in Boston while I'm working remotely."

"I'm kind of surprised Diane let you work remotely." He leaned forward in his chair, closer to her.

She leaned back in hers, farther from him. "I didn't give her much choice. And I swear she texts me and emails me a million times a day. Or night."

"As I remember, Diane lives and dies by her job. I think her job is like her oxygen that keeps her alive."

"She hasn't changed any. She's still all work, all the time. I usually am too, but... well, Aunt Lil needs me, and she was there for me when I needed her."

"I'm sure it's a great relief for her knowing you're here helping to keep the inn running smoothly while she's away."

"I'm not sure I'd call it smoothly. I'd never have been able to do it without Robin and Charlotte's help. I just hope we're not screwing anything up. Well, nothing major." She grinned.

"I'm sure you're doing fine." He nodded encouragingly.

"Charlotte is doing a fantastic job with the

remodel of two of the cottages. And I think she's enjoying doing it."

"You said she was an artist if I remember right."

"You remember correctly. She is. She lives in California. She's having some kind of painter's block thing going on, so I think she likes the creative outlet of fixing up the cabin."

He sat there listening intently. He'd always been such a great listener. But now she wanted to know about him.

"So, how about you? What's been going on with you in the last… oh, twenty years or so?"

His lips curled in a warm smile. "Well, there was raising Zoe, of course. That was quite an adventure. I knew nothing about kids, much less one who had lost both her parents. It was really tough at first. I took a couple of months just to sort out everything and be there for Zoe. Eventually, I had to go back to work. Didn't have much trouble finding another job in advertising. Diane's pretty well known in the industry and I think she gave me a great recommendation."

"That's good."

"It was good and bad. It was a large agency, and the hours were grueling. Luckily I still had the same lady my sister had found—Marisol—to watch Zoe. She stuck around even after Zoe started school."

"How old was Zoe when your sister... when you started looking after her?"

"She was three, just about four."

"Wow, that was young."

"And I was clueless. So clueless." He shrugged. "Luckily, Marisol stuck around and would be there for Zoe when she got out of school. But the job got even crazier, lots of evenings and weekends. I tried to balance the job and Zoe and tried not to miss any of her games or things at her school. But... well, I wasn't very good at it. Actually, I was *terrible* at it. If I left work to see one of Zoe's games, I felt guilty I wasn't at work. If I had to work and miss something at her school, I felt guilty I wasn't there for her."

"I'm sure it was hard being a single parent."

"I finally took Zoe on vacation and decided to come to Belle Island. You always made it sound like a magical place. I needed that back then. We got here, and she ran around on the beach, we spent hours together, and she was just so happy. Happier than I'd seen her since my sister died." He reached and took a sip of his wine. "She made a friend that week here—Lisa — and begged to stay. So, I kind of just decided that we'd up and move here. Give Zoe the small-town life. Find a job where I could be around for her. They happened to have the community center director's job open, and I suggested some advertising and promotion for them and... well, I got the job. And Lisa and Zoe are still best friends."

"So just like that you packed up and moved? To *my* island?"

He grinned. "*Your* island. Yes, pretty much. And Zoe thrived here. Made friends immediately. Quit being this sad, serious kid and just... well, it was rewarding to see I'd made the right decision."

Sara had a hard time processing all the changes in Noah's life. How he'd taken on raising his niece and given up a promising career to move here to the island so he could spend more time with her. She reached across the table and took his hand. "You're a good man, Noah McNeil."

He gave her a soft smile. "Thank you. That means a lot to me."

"You gave up so much for her."

"I'd do it again in a heartbeat. She gave a lot

to me, too. I learned from her. She's the best thing that ever happened to me."

"I am sorry about your sister and brother-in-law. Accident?"

"Yes, just a random two-car accident. You don't think that will ever happen… and then it does." He looked out the window, then back at her. "Anyway, Zoe is great. She has a job up near Orlando now. I miss her, but I guess everyone has to let their kids spread their wings at some time."

She didn't miss the look in his eyes. How much he cared about Zoe, how hard it was to let her go. She squeezed his hand again.

"I still can't believe you chose Belle Island. Weren't you afraid you'd run into me?"

"Kind of. But the town rumors were that you rarely came back. And Zoe loved it here so much. I'd always choose Zoe's happiness over worrying about feeling awkward running into you."

The waitress came with their dinner and she slipped her hand back but suddenly missed the connection to Noah.

After dinner, Noah suggested a walk on the beach. She looked around and saw only a few tables that still held customers, so she agreed. "A walk sounds like a nice idea."

They headed outside and down to the beach. The sun was just beginning to slip behind a ledge of fluffy clouds out over the water. She loved this time of the evening, with the breeze blowing and the colorful sunset sky.

They walked along the beach toward the lighthouse, which was washed in a golden glow from the sunset.

"I think the lighthouse is magical, too." Noah's words surprised her.

"What?"

"You always talked about how much you loved the lighthouse, almost like it was a living, breathing part of your life. Now that I've been here, I can see the draw. She's a beaut, isn't she?"

"I do love it. It's just always there. Strong. Protective. Withstanding the storms."

"Have you ever made a wish at Lighthouse Point? I've heard the town legend that if you make a wish on the point and throw a shell in the water, your wish comes true."

She grinned. "That's just a silly old legend."

"Is it?" He eyed her.

"Yes, it is. I don't believe in that stuff."

He reached down and picked up a shell, closed his eyes for a second, and tossed the shell into the sea.

"Wait, did you just make a wish?" She stared at him in amazement. The Noah she knew wouldn't believe in that kind of nonsense. But then, maybe she didn't know this new Noah...

"Might have."

"What did you wish for?"

"Can't tell you. It won't come true." He shrugged.

She shook her head. "You're crazy, you know that?"

"Maybe."

He reached over and slipped her hand in his. She stood there looking at their hands, their fingers entwined. He smiled, turned, and led her back down the beach toward the inn.

The sun slipped below the horizon, tossing brilliant orange and yellow hues across the clouds floating above them. A swath of purple clung to the horizon. They paused for a moment watching nature's glorious display.

"It's beautiful." She whispered the words so as not to disturb the beauty around them.

He turned and looked directly at her. "Beautiful."

Noah liked the feeling of Sara's hand in his. Liked talking with her. Liked... well, he'd liked every single detail about this evening. They reached the inn and climbed the steps to a back wing.

"This is what Aunt Lil and I call The Nest. It's our little wing of the inn." She opened the door. "Do you want to come in for a little bit?"

Yes, yes he did. Quite a bit, actually. He didn't want the night to end. "Sure."

They went inside and he took in the comfortable furnishings. All picked up and organized, just like Lil. He crossed the room and picked up a photograph. "Is this you?"

Sara grinned. "It was. All gawky with braids and braces."

He smiled and set the photo down.

"Would you like a glass of wine out on the deck?"

He glanced at his watch. It was getting late for him, but he didn't care. "Yes, that would be nice." Tonight seemed like as good a night as any to break his early to bed, early to rise routine he'd gotten into since Zoe left. The nights were just so... quiet... now without her.

They took their wine outside and settled onto a loveseat rocker. A low light from a solar lantern cast a cozy glow around them. A cool breeze stirred the tangy night air.

"I had a nice time tonight." He turned to look at her.

"I did, too." She gave him a small smile.

He'd missed that smile. One side of her mouth always seemed to tilt up more and her eyes sparkled when she smiled. He reached over and covered her hand. He wanted that connection to her again.

"Noah?"

"Hm?"

"I… I've missed you."

That shocked him. He'd always figured she hadn't even thought of him over the years. He'd thought of her often, though. Very often. "I missed you, too. Missed talking with you. Laughing with you."

And he'd missed kissing her. He'd really missed that.

She looked up at him with that crooked smile and he almost—*almost*—leaned over to kiss her.

But he didn't.

CHAPTER 18

Sara got up early the next morning and sat at the table in The Nest with her laptop open and a full cup of coffee to get her motivated. She had to finish this presentation. She actually thought she'd come up with a pretty good idea for the campaign. Very different from the ideas they'd presented before. She still needed to get the presentation slides ready, but she had time. It didn't need to be to Diane until this evening.

She took a sip of the hot coffee. She'd stayed up past midnight talking to Noah and she was dragging a bit this morning. She stood and crossed over to the window, looking out at the deck and the crystal blue water beyond it. What a night it had been. She'd actually thought he was going to kiss her at one point.

But he hadn't.

And she didn't know how she felt about that.

And she'd almost kissed him when he left... but she hadn't quite worked up the nerve.

Her phone dinged, and she sighed. Diane.

Last day. I need the presentation by five.

As if she didn't remember that fact. Diane had texted the deadline to her like ten times. Time to get back to work. She returned to her chair, determined to bang out the rest of the presentation and get it to Diane. Early, if possible.

Her phone rang later and she glanced at the clock. Where had the time gone? It was almost noon. She almost ignored the call, sure it was Diane with something else that just had to be said right this minute. She sighed, reached for the phone, and frowned. Not Diane. But a local area code.

"Hello?"

"Sara, this is Ashley Harden."

"Dr. Harden, is everything okay?" Her pulse began to race.

"It's Lil. She's spiked a fever and the rehab place called me. The fever is pretty high and we're doing everything we can to bring it down. It's probably a virus, but I'm running some blood tests to be sure. We're a bit worried it might settle in her lungs. She's developed quite a cough. I worry about complications such as pneumonia when the patient isn't very mobile. I thought you'd want to know."

She snapped shut the laptop. "I'll be there as soon as I can."

"I don't want to alarm you, but she looks very weak. The staff here said she had a rough night."

"I'm coming right now."

She grabbed her purse and hurried through to the inn to find Jay. He was standing near the stove and Robin was lounging against the counter beside him. "I have to leave. Aunt Lil isn't feeling well. She has a high fever they're trying to break."

Robin pushed off the counter. "Go, go. We've got everything covered here. Don't worry about a thing."

She gave Robin a quick hug. "Thanks. I don't know what I'd do without you. You're the best."

"Hey, what about me?" Jay teased her.

"You're the best, too, Jay." She assured him. "Seriously, we'd never have been able to keep everything running without you."

"Good thing I had my coffee." He pointed to his t-shirt. *First coffee… then I'm awesome.*

She grinned. "Good thing."

"So, go. Get out of here." Jay waved a spatula in the direction of the door.

"Call me and let me know how Lil's doing." Robin walked her over to the doorway.

"I will." She hurried out to her car and drove to the rehab center. She rushed inside and hurried down the hallway to Aunt Lil's room.

Dr. Harden stood at Lil's bedside. Sara nodded to her and crossed over to Lil.

"She's sleeping now. I'm hoping the meds we gave her will break the fever."

Aunt Lil's face was flushed a rosy red and her hair was damp. "I just saw her yesterday."

"She started feeling badly around dinner time and then last night her fever spiked."

She reached over and smoothed the damp locks away from Aunt Lil's face.

"If she wakes up, see if you can get her to take a few sips of water. You can put a cool cloth on her forehead to see if that helps. I'll check in later today."

"Thanks, Doctor."

"Please, call me Ashley. I consider Lil my friend."

Sara nodded.

Ashley left the room and Sara dragged a chair to her aunt's beside. A rough cough wracked Lil's body and she moaned.

"Ah, Aunt Lil. You're having such a tough time of it. Don't worry about anything. I'm here and the inn is fine. You just get better." A lone tear trailed down Sara's cheek. Aunt Lil looked so… fragile.

Charlotte sat back on her heels, eyeing the table she'd just finished painting. It had turned out pretty nice if she did say so herself. She'd painted it a dark teal as a base, then layered a pale teal on top. There were so many lovely shades of teal, some more green, some more blue. She loved playing with the shading and blending. When the top layer dried, she planned on sanding it to let some of the darker color show through. She planned on painting the two chairs with yet another shade of teal. Then she'd have to seal all of them.

She'd really enjoyed this chance to use her creativity with no pressure. No one saying she needed to come up with a new idea, a new concept. She just… painted.

The door swung open and Robin came into the cottage. "I thought I might find you here at the teal cottage. Hey, that looks really great."

Charlotte stood, paintbrush in hand. "Thank you. I'm fairly pleased. Maybe I should change my career and paint furniture for a living."

Robin shrugged. "If it makes you happy, you should. But I think you're a fabulous, talented artist. You can do anything you want with your talents."

She grinned. "You always were my biggest fan."

"I don't know. Lil is always touting your talents, too." Robin frowned. "Lil's not doing well. She's running a fever. Sara headed to the mainland."

"That's not good."

"No, it's not. Lil is having a rough go of it. I hope she fights this off and gets back to her perky self."

She walked over to the sink to clean her brush. "Let me get things cleaned up here, and I can come over to the inn to help out wherever you need me."

"We can use you in the dining room. I swear, we've got to get more help hired. We have some interviews scheduled this afternoon. Hope someone works out."

"I'm here to help where I can. I almost feel like Lil is my aunt too."

"I hear you. I spent more time here at The Nest or the inn growing up than my own house."

She smiled. "Those were some great times, great memories."

"We'll make more. We just need to get Lil all fixed up and better." Robin grinned. "And make sure the inn is still standing when she gets back."

Noah clicked on his email and scanned through them. One of them caught his eye. It was from a retirement village near Orlando where he'd sent his resume. Just two days ago after Zoe's urging. It had seemed like such a great idea at the time, but now he wasn't sure...

But it wouldn't hurt to take an interview.

Besides, what was keeping him here in Belle Island when Zoe was in Orlando? He had his job and his friends, but no family here.

He picked up the phone and called to arrange to go there and talk to them about the job. Besides, it would give him a chance to see Zoe. He sent her a text to see if she could meet up with him after the interview.

He stood and walked over to the window of his office. The fronds on the palm tree danced in the breeze from the incoming storm that was predicted to blow in from sea today.

He'd hate leaving the island, though. It had become home to him. He'd raised Zoe here and learned to... what? Live? Relax? Take time to just enjoy the simple things. He walked back over to the desk, toying with calling them back and saying he wasn't interested.

But he'd already texted Zoe that he was coming up. He'd at least go and hear about the position. Maybe a more challenging job would be good for him now. And Zoe sounded like she truly would love to have him closer.

And if he was being honest, part of the allure of the island right now was Sara. And she'd be leaving soon.

He raked his hand through his hair. Why hadn't he kissed her last night? He'd wanted to. But then he'd thought it would make it all more complicated.

How did his simple life get this perplexing? Sara coming back in his life. A possible move and new job. Was it really just a week ago when he could just sit back and enjoy his simple, predictable life?

He sighed and sank onto his chair. Maybe they wouldn't even offer him a job, and then he wouldn't have to decide.

He grabbed the file where he'd jotted notes about next month's calendar for the community center and started to add the events onto the center's website. This was familiar. He knew how to do this. He grinned when he saw the town's bake-off competition coming up. He loved judging that one!

Sara looked up as the door swung open to Aunt Lil's room. Noah stood in the doorway, a sack in one hand, a cup in the other. Her heart did a quick flip-flop at the sight of him. She rose from her chair, careful not to make any noise, and crossed the room. "What are you doing here?" she asked in a hushed voice.

"Ran into Robin and she said Lil wasn't doing well. She was worried you hadn't eaten all day."

She gave him a small smile. "She'd be right."

"So, I brought you dinner from the inn. Jay packed you up a meal." He handed her the sack.

"You didn't need to come all the way over to the mainland."

"I was worried about you, too." He reached out and touched her shoulder and turned her around. "Sit and eat."

She did as she was told and nibbled on the roast beef sandwich Jay had sent. She was hungry, but her stomach was in knots, worrying about Aunt Lil.

Noah stood beside the bed looking down at Lil. "She's a tough one, you know. She'll kick this."

"She will," Sara said as more of a wish than an affirmation.

"Noah, is that you?" Aunt Lil opened her eyes.

Sara jumped up. "You're awake."

Lil reached up and touched the cloth on her forehead, then another cough swept through her, shaking her body. "Ah…"

"Do you want a sip of water?" She reached for the cup beside the bed.

Aunt Lil nodded, took a sip of the offered water, then leaned back against the pillows.

Sara reached out and touched Aunt Lil's face. It felt cooler.

A nurse entered the room. "I'm going to check on Lil now if you two want to wait outside for a few minutes."

She and Noah went out in the hallway. "I appreciate you bringing me dinner."

"Just wanted to check on you." He reached out and squeezed her hand.

She clung to him for a moment, grateful for the support and the connection. She swirled in feelings of abandonment with fears of losing Aunt Lil.

"It's going to be okay." His low voice washed over her, giving her hope and strength. "Do you want me to stay with you?"

As much as she wanted to say yes, she didn't. She had enough friends doing things for her now. Helping with the inn and supporting her. Noah didn't need to think of her as another responsibility. "No, I'm fine. You go on back to the island. But thank you for coming."

He wrapped one arm around her in a half-hug. "Take care."

Then his arm was gone, and she watched while he walked away down the hallway. He turned and waved before he turned the corner. She waved back and leaned against the wall, exhausted.

The nurse came out in the hall. "Her fever has broken. Hopefully, we can keep it that way."

"Oh, that's good news." She went back into the room. Aunt Lil was already sound asleep. Which was good. That's what she needed.

She sank into the chair and took a few more bites of her dinner and sipped on the soda while she watched the uneven rise and fall of Aunt Lil's chest as she struggled with her breathing.

She stayed until late and Aunt Lil's fever still hadn't returned. The nurse at the rehab center told her to go home and promised to call if there was any change.

She walked out to her car, taking in deep breaths of the cool air. She looked at her watch. It was way past when Diane told her to turn in the presentation, but she was going to go home and finish it and send it in. It was a good idea.

One of her best. Diane would still have time to read through it before her meeting with Coastal Furniture.

Though, the string of texts that had come into her phone this evening had shown her how mad Diane was that she'd missed the deadline. The first time she'd ever missed a deadline since she'd started working for the agency.

But that didn't matter as much to her as it probably should have. All she'd wanted to do today was to be by Aunt Lil's side.

CHAPTER 19

The next morning, after three hours of sleep and a rough start, Sara whirled around in the kitchen, looking for her cell phone. Its persistent ring taunted her. Where was it? There it was. Half under a stack of papers where she'd jotted notes last night. She snatched it up.

"We didn't get the account." Diane's voice was frosty cold.

No hello. No good morning. Nothing. "Really?" Sara juggled her phone and a cup of coffee. "I thought my idea would really appeal to them." She'd only gotten a few hours of sleep but had managed to send the presentation to Diane around two in the morning. That would have given Diane plenty of time to read through it before the ten a.m. meeting with the client.

"I didn't present your idea. I presented Terrence's. He had it to me yesterday afternoon, and we had time to tweak and fine-tune it. And since you couldn't be here to give the pitch, I went with his idea."

Terrence rarely came up with creative ideas, so she wasn't surprised they didn't get the account.

"Did you look at my idea?"

"Didn't have to, I already had Terrence's." Diane's words were dismissive.

"You know, Diane, I had a great idea for them. I did. But you were angry that I couldn't get it sent until late last night, past the deadline you gave me. But my aunt will always come first." Or she would from now on. No more putting off visits. "I think they would have gone for my idea. It was really good if I do say so myself, and I'm sorry you chose to pitch Terrence's."

"His was in by my deadline."

"But the customer didn't like it."

Diane was silent for once.

"Diane, when Noah McNeil left the company all those years ago. Back when I got my first promotion. He gave you a note for me. You never gave it to me."

"I—" Silence filled the air. "I didn't want you to know I offered the job to him first. I figured he'd call you soon enough and you'd find out. But I wanted you to be excited about the promotion."

Not a good enough excuse. Not at all. Suddenly she just didn't care about Diane, Terrence, the Coastal account, or the agency.

"Diane, I'll need to work remotely for a while longer. If you don't want me to do that, I've accrued months of vacation. I can take that if you prefer. I'll be back in the office as soon as I can. I need to get Aunt Lil settled back at home as soon as she's ready. I'll talk to you soon." And Sara Wren who never rocked the boat, who never stood up for herself to Diane, hung up the phone.

She sank down on the chair, a bit shaky, but proud of herself. No client was worth not being there for Aunt Lil. She'd probably lost any chance at the promotion. Between missing the deadline and now standing up to Diane... there wasn't any chance at all. Terrence would get the promotion.

She stood and paced the floor. Did she care

that she'd lost her chance? Yes, she did. She still wanted that partner position. But not if it meant scurrying back to Boston and leaving Aunt Lil to fend for herself.

She set her coffee cup in the sink and grabbed her keys. She needed to run over to the mainland and check on Aunt Lil. Ashley had called this morning to say Aunt Lil was much better when she'd been in to check on her. But she wanted to see that for herself.

She grabbed her phone and put it on silent. No interruptions from Diane. Though Diane may never speak to her again. She half-expected to receive a termination letter in her email.

But none of that mattered right now. She just wanted time with Aunt Lil.

Sara found Robin and Charlotte at the yellow cottage that afternoon, sipping sweet tea on the porch.

"I'll grab another glass." Charlotte jumped up and retrieved another glass from the cottage.

Sara sank into one of the worn and oh-so-comfortable wooden chairs. The lack of sleep and the emotional stress was getting to her.

She rolled her shoulders forward and backward.

"How's Lil?" Robin asked.

"She's much better today. She was sitting up in bed sipping some soup. Her cough is a little better. Her fever hasn't come back."

"That's great news." Charlotte sat in the chair beside her. "Lil's tough. She'll be fine soon. Just you see."

"I hope so. I hate seeing her looking so... weak."

"Even at her worst, Lil is not weak. Toughest person I know." Robin turned and looked at her. "But you, my friend, you look terrible."

"Gee, thanks." She took a sip of the icy liquid. "Oh, this is good."

"Char made it. Who knew she had hidden talents of sweet tea making?"

"Maybe she can teach me. Maybe I can become a professional tea maker because it looks like I might have lost my job."

Charlotte set down her glass, leaned over, and took her hand. "Oh, no. What happened?"

"I came home from the hospital last night and turned in the pitch for Coastal Furniture. But it was late. Diane wanted it by five and it was like two a.m. when I sent it. Though Diane gets up about four or five every morning, so I figured she'd still have time to read it."

"Did she like it?" Robin cocked her head.

"I have no clue if she even read it. She went with Terrence's idea. He's this guy who works at the agency. Not too creative but he's always working some angle. Anyway, they didn't get the client. She's furious."

"I'm sorry." Charlotte's eyes filled with sympathy.

"I *was* late. Now I'm fairly certain I'm out of the running for partner. And I might have given a piece of my mind to Diane, told her I was either taking vacation or working remotely until I got Aunt Lil settled back at The Nest." She grinned. "Then, I *might* have just hung up my phone instead of letting her yell at me."

"Good for you." Robin raised her drink and the three of them clinked glasses. "Always knew you had it in you."

CHAPTER 20

Noah called Robin to see how Aunt Lil and Sara were doing and found out that Sara was back at the inn.

He should go over and check on her. It was the neighborly, nice thing to do, right? Friends check in on friends when they're going through a rough time. That's all this was.

"Come on, Coop. Wanna go for a walk?"

The Aussie stood, stretched, and sauntered over to the door with an are-you-coming look.

"Hey, it was *my* idea." He crossed to the door, and they walked out. The sun was low in the sky and the promised storm clouds gathered in the distance. He debated changing his mind and driving over, but Cooper could use the walk. Well, so could he. He'd done nothing but sit at his desk all day doing paperwork and making phone calls.

He headed down the sidewalk toward the inn. They walked around to the back and he spied Sara sitting on the deck, staring out at the sea, lost in thought. He almost turned around to leave her with her thoughts, but Cooper went bounding up the steps.

She broke into a grin and threw her arms around Coop's neck. "Hey, there, buddy."

Noah climbed the stairs and Sara turned to him and gave him one of her smiles. The smiles that did something to him. Made his heart pound and his pulse race. Made him feel special.

Made him...

...want to kiss her.

"Well, this is just what I needed." She petted Cooper.

"To be mauled by my dog?" He grinned at her.

"I'm becoming quite fond of your dog."

That was a step in the right direction... He caught himself just short of asking 'what about me?'

"I could pop inside and grab us a couple of beers." She started to stand.

"I'll get them." He headed inside, found two bottles of beer in the fridge, twisted their caps off, and headed back outside. He sat in the chair beside her and handed her a bottle.

She clinked hers against his, then took a sip. "Ah, that's good."

He took a swig of his and settled back in his chair. "You looked lost in thought when we got here."

"I was thinking about Lil. How she took me in when I was so young. She knew nothing about raising a kid, but she gave up everything for me." Sara looked at him. "Just like you did with Zoe."

"I didn't really have any choice." He shrugged.

"Aunt Lil probably felt the same way. There was no one else. But she never complained." She sighed. "I hope she gets better soon."

"She will."

Sara turned to look out at the sea again. "Looks like we're going to get that storm they've predicted all day." A streak of lightning flashed behind the clouds in the distance.

"Looks like it."

"Aunt Lil and I used to sit out here and watch the storms roll in. Listen for the rumble of thunder. Count the seconds between the flashes of lightning and the clap of thunder. We'd stay out here until the last possible moment, then rush inside at the first splattering of rain." She let out a long breath. "I have such great childhood memories, and Aunt Lil made sure that I did. You'd think a girl who lost her parents would say she had a terrible childhood. But I didn't. I mean, I missed my parents. Missed them a lot. But Aunt Lil made me feel safe. Loved. Protected. Anyway, I was very lucky to have her."

He watched her face, mesmerized. The sweep of her eyelashes. The hint of a smile tugging at her lips. The wisps of hair tossing around on the breeze.

Unaware he was staring at her, she started counting under her breath with the next flash of lightning.

"Six." She grinned. "Pretty close."

Cooper got up and walked over to the railing, peering out through the posts.

She set her hand on the armrest and he reached over and covered her hand. They sat and watched the flashes of lightning light up the sky.

Before long, large drops of rain started to

splatter around them. Cooper turned and looked at them as if they were crazy.

Sara jumped up. "Come on, we better get inside." The rain slashed down on them.

"Cooper, come." The dog raced past him and squeezed in the doorway with Sara. Noah was right on their heels.

Sara walked into the kitchen area, acutely aware of Noah's presence. She swallowed. "Um, would you like another beer? It appears we left our last ones out in the storm."

He nodded.

She walked over to the fridge and tugged it open. The cool air rushed over her dampened skin. Goosebumps crept across her arms and legs. She grabbed two beers and set them on the counter, looking for the bottle opener. She was horrible at twisting off the caps with her hands.

"I've got it." Noah reached out for the bottles and twisted off one cap, then the other. He handed one to her and their fingers brushed. She took a quick sip of the beer, then licked her lips.

Noah was making her so nervous, which was silly. He was an old friend. Nothing more.

Cooper stood between them and looked from one of them to the other. With a brief wave of his tail, he trotted over and settled down in front of the sliding door, resting his head on his paws, and staring outside at the storm.

She turned away from Noah and headed for the couch. He followed, sat down next to her, and stretched out his long legs. She leaned against the back of the couch and Noah draped an arm casually around her shoulder. It took all her willpower to not just scoot over and cuddle against him like she had so many times all those years ago.

Noah was staring out the window, lost in thought, a slight frown on his face.

"What are you thinking about?"

He turned to her and gave her a brief smile. "Zoe. She was so afraid of storms when she was little. She'd cover her ears when it thundered. She finally outgrew her fear. Or at least I think she did. Or she hid it from me as she got older." He frowned again. "As she got older, she started taking care of me. Learned to cook and made most of our dinners. She's always worrying about me now."

"She cares about you."

He shrugged. "But she shouldn't worry about me."

"We always worry about the people we care about."

He looked directly at her. "Yes, you're right. We do."

But somehow she got the feeling he wasn't talking about Zoe. He pulled her closer to his side and she leaned against him.

So familiar.

So strange.

He ran his hand slowly up and down her arm. Contentment swept through her as they sat and watched the storm in silence. She relaxed, safely protected in Noah's arms.

Noah looked down at Sara, sleeping peacefully in his arms. He wasn't sure when she'd fallen asleep exactly, but somewhere between talking and watching the storm, she'd drifted off.

He brushed a lock of hair away from her face and she murmured in her sleep. He should probably go…

But still, he sat there and held her, enjoying

feeling her beside him. It was probably a crazy thing to start dating Sara. He lived here… or possibly near Orlando if he did find a new job and move. She lived in Boston. Or would after Lil got back to the inn and got settled again.

She shifted closer to him in her sleep.

He could sit like this all night.

And, yet, he couldn't. With a long sigh, he slowly loosened his hold on her and she slipped down on the couch, with her head on the pillow he placed for her. He lifted the quilt off the back of the couch and draped it over her. Sleep was what she needed.

He nodded to Cooper who stood, stretched, and trotted over to him. They went into the kitchen and he found a piece of paper.

You fell asleep and I let myself out. Hope you got a good night's sleep. I'll talk to you tomorrow. Thanks for the beer and the…

What did he want to say? Obviously she'd know she fell asleep. He crumbled the note and started again.

. . .

Had a good time tonight. I let myself out. Talk to you in the morning.

Noah

There was so much more he'd like to say to her, but he didn't. And even if he did want to say more to her, it would be in person, not in a note. Or a phone message. He'd never make that mistake again.

He and Cooper slipped out the door. A light misty rain was falling, but he didn't really mind. "Come on, Coop. Let's go home." They headed down the sidewalk and he couldn't help whistling a tune under his breath.

CHAPTER 21

Sara awoke on the couch with the sun streaming in the window. She looked around, confused for a moment. The last thing she remembered was talking with Noah. She must have fallen asleep. She sat up, stretched, and moved her neck from side to side to work out the crick from sleeping on the couch.

Craving coffee, she stood and went to the kitchen. She found the note from Noah and smiled at his familiar handwriting. How many times had they sat at a table scribbling notes about some client's project? She set the note on the counter, smoothing it carefully.

She made the coffee and went to shower while it brewed. Soon she was back and pouring her treasured cup of the velvety liquid. Yes, she needed her morning coffee.

She took the cup and walked barefoot out on the deck. Fluffy clouds dotted the sky, and there were no signs of last night's storm except for a few palm fronds that had dropped to the ground in the winds.

She walked down the worn wooden stairs and crossed the beach, standing at the edge of the water. The waves rolled in with a constant rhythm that soothed her soul. How could she have stayed away so long? She'd almost forgotten how restoring the water could be.

A group of pelicans flew by above her. She lifted her face to the warmth of the sun.

Her phone rang, and she slipped it from her pocket, unlocking it with a quick slide of her thumb. "Hello?"

"Sara, it's Ashley."

"Is Aunt Lil okay?"

"Better than okay. She is chomping at the bit to come home. She's a tough one. I told her two more days. But I wanted to give you a heads-up so you can get things ready."

"That's great news."

"She'll need to only walk for brief periods

of time at first, and she'll need to use a walker for a while."

"I bet she's thrilled with that."

"I told her she'll have to be patient with the healing. I don't want her to do stairs. Is that going to be a problem?"

Sara frowned. "No, I'll figure something out." Aunt Lil could use the ramp that the inn had on one entrance, but then it would be a long walk to The Nest.

"Okay, good. So I'll set her release up for Saturday morning."

"Perfect. Tell Aunt Lil I'll be in to see her later today."

"I will."

Sara slipped her phone back into her pocket, took her last sip of coffee, and headed back to The Nest. Lots to do to get things ready, but she was happy her aunt was coming home.

After she finished getting ready, she went off in search of Jay. She found him in the kitchen, chatting with Robin while he cooked. "Hey, guys."

Robin turned around. "Sara, hi. Wow, you look better this morning. Must have gotten a good night's sleep."

"I'm not sure if I should take that as a

compliment." She grinned at Robin. "But I did sleep well. And guess what? Aunt Lil's coming home Saturday."

"That's great news." Jay grabbed a tray of cinnamon rolls from the oven. "Want one?" He motioned to the rolls with his spatula.

"You bet." Sara grabbed a plate. "Robin?"

"Yep, me, too."

Sara grabbed a second plate and Jay slipped cinnamon rolls onto each one. She lounged against the counter while she waited for the roll to cool a bit.

The kitchen door swung open and Noah poked his head in. "Thought I might find you here when you weren't at The Nest."

A wide smile spread across her face. Robin caught it and looked at her pointedly. She shrugged at Robin.

"Come in. Jay's feeding us cinnamon rolls."

"Count me in." He looked at Jay. "Nice shirt."

Jay glanced down at his shirt. *I like coffee, my dog… and maybe two people.* "Yep, and I'm afraid it's true."

"I was just telling Robin and Jay that Aunt Lil is coming home Saturday."

"I bet she's more than ready."

"Anyway, Ashley said no stairs for Aunt Lil. And limited walking."

Jay frowned. "We have the ramp on that one entrance but—"

"I know. That's a long way from The Nest." Sara nodded. "And I'm not thinking she'll agree to a wheelchair."

"I could make a ramp for the stairs to The Nest. A long, gentle slope," Noah offered.

She looked at him doubtfully. "You know how to build stuff?"

He laughed. "I do. I've learned lots since I left the advertising business. I've built stage props and I even built a dollhouse for Zoe when she was little."

What other surprises was Noah hiding? Every time she turned around she found out something new about the man.

"I can help you this afternoon," Jay offered.

"Great. I'll get the lumber and bring over some tools."

"Wow, I know I keep saying this, but you guys are helping me so much."

Jay shrugged. "Nah, it's helping Lil. Anyway, it's no big deal." Jay waved a spatula at all of them. "Now, take those rolls out to the dining room and grab some coffee. I've got work to do."

"Okay, okay. We'll get out of your hair." Sara led them out of the kitchen and they settled at a table by the window.

"He makes the best cinnamon rolls." Robin took a big bite.

"He does. I remember that much." Sara tried hers. "Yes, just like I remembered."

"If I ate Jay's cooking all the time, I'd gain a zillion pounds." Robin shrugged and took another bite. She quickly finished her roll and stood. "I better run. I've got to put in another order for Jay."

Sara got the distinct feeling Robin was just using that as an excuse to leave her alone with Noah…

And she didn't really mind that…

"Might have to take another walk to work off this cinnamon roll." Noah patted his stomach.

They finished their rolls and sat sipping their coffee.

"Sorry about falling asleep on you last night." She set her mug down.

"Not a problem. I was afraid I might wake

you up when Coop and I left, but you were really out of it."

"I was tired. I'd been up most of the night before working on a presentation for Diane." She shook her head. "But Diane didn't even read it. It was late. She went with Terrence's proposal and they ended up not getting the account. Coastal Furniture. I had a really great idea for them."

"Diane is a stickler for deadlines."

"I know, but Aunt Lil spiked that fever, and I needed to be with her. I guess I should have brought my laptop with me to the hospital, but I was so worried when they called, I just rushed out the door to see her." She fiddled with the salt and pepper shakers, putting them carefully in alignment. "And that promotion I told you I was up for? I'm pretty sure this shot all my chances of that."

"You don't know that for sure."

"I told her it was too bad she didn't use my idea because it was one of my better ideas. *Then*, I kind of told her I had accrued vacation—lots of it—and I would either be taking it or I could work remotely. *Then…*" She grinned. "I clicked off my cell phone and didn't give her a chance to yell at me."

"You did?" His eyes widened in surprise.

"I did. And you know what? It felt good. I did come up with a great proposal, and even if it *was* late, it was there in time for her to use. And they lost the account with Terrence's idea. Let's just say he's not the most creative person they've hired."

"So have you heard from Diane since?"

"Nope, not a text, not an email all day yesterday."

"That's probably a welcome break." He grinned at her.

"It was." She sighed. "I guess I'm officially taking that vacation since she hasn't sent me another project to work on. I have roughly a bazillion vacation days accrued."

"You never were one to take many days off."

"And it only got worse. I rarely even took weekends off."

"That's no way to live." He looked at her with concern in his eyes.

"Now that I'm back here on Belle Island, I'm beginning to realize that."

"Good. But then you'd actually have to do something about it." He pinned her with a gaze that would have rivaled one of Robin's listen-to-me gazes.

"Okay, okay. I'll make some changes."

"Good. Now how about if I go get the supplies for the ramp, and you can meet me back at The Nest after lunch? I have to check on a few things at the community center, too. I'll teach you how to build a ramp."

She looked at him doubtfully. "I've never swung a hammer or used a saw. You sure you want my help?"

"I'm a great teacher. I'll see you then." Noah stood, took one more sip of his coffee, and hurried off.

He crossed the dining room with confident, long strides. This new Noah was quite the enigma.

Lil stood at the window in the room at the rehab center. She looked out on the courtyard dotted with palm trees. A cheerful fountain splashed in the courtyard and residents more mobile than she was wandered around in the sunshine.

She was ready to go home. Enough time in the hospital and rehab with people coming in constantly to check on her. She was fine. Or she would be fine if people would just leave her alone.

It felt like an eternity since she'd been back on her beloved Belle Island and at the inn. And the sooner she got back, the sooner Sara could get back to Boston and her real life. She didn't want her niece sacrificing for her.

She really should consider getting a manager for the inn who could help with the day-to-day running of things. As they expanded and the dining room grew larger and busier, both she and Jay had their hands full.

She'd work on that as soon as they let her out of here. She didn't know why Ashley had insisted on two more days of therapy. She felt fine now… if a little bit tired.

She sighed and turned away from the window, using the silly walker they insisted she use, and walked over to the recliner. She carefully lowered herself into the chair, ignoring the twinges of pain.

She needed to be up and mobile. Exercising her muscles, getting stronger. She wasn't ready for some kind of fragile period of life. She had years of vibrant life yet and she planned on living them to the fullest.

Only old ladies broke their hip, and she

refused to consider herself an old lady. So she'd ignore it and get stronger. Soon she could put this whole silly episode behind her and things would get back to normal.

She needed that. Craved that. Normal.

She sighed when an overly cheerful worker came bustling into the room.

"So, how are we doing today?"

We are doing just peachy if *we* could just get out of here.

But she smiled and replied, "Just fine."

CHAPTER 22

Sara checked on the progress of the yellow cottage and the teal cottage. The teal one was just about finished. Charlotte had done a great job with everything.

She walked back to The Nest and climbed the stairs, trying to figure out how Noah was going to make a ramp work. Oh well, he sounded confident in his abilities. She'd just let him have at it.

She walked inside and heard noise from the direction of the sunroom. She went to investigate. Charlotte stood in front of a blank easel. She'd spread a drop cloth on the floor and had a selection of paints and brushes on a small table beside her.

She entered the brightly lit room and

Charlotte turned and gave her a weak smile. "So… it's not really working well for me just yet." She nodded at the blank canvas.

"I'm sure something will come to you soon. Something will inspire you."

"I hope so. I thought maybe coming here and getting away would. Or all the work I'm doing on painting the furniture for the cottages might help."

"You're doing such a great job on those. Aunt Lil is going to be so pleased."

"I hope so. I've had a lot of fun with them. Did you see the nautical compass I stenciled on the top of that dresser in the teal cottage?"

"I did. And did you letter that *beach this way* sign?"

"I did. I had some leftover paint, found those boards, and painted them. I think it tied together the colors I used, don't you?"

"It's wonderful. I can't thank you enough for all your work."

"I'm really enjoying myself."

"I'm glad." Sara hugged Charlotte. "Now, we'll just have to work on your painter's block."

"I hope so." Charlotte glanced at the canvas. "Enough of this. I've got a second coat of paint to put on the chairs at the teal cottage."

"Oh, hey. Aunt Lil is coming home on Saturday."

"That's great."

"And this afternoon Noah and Jay are going to make a temporary ramp for her to use."

"Always good to have handymen around. I'll come help, too. I've done my fair share of basic carpentry."

"You have?" Was she the only person on the island who didn't know how to paint, how to build, or how to cook? What was she good at besides coming up with ideas for clients? She frowned.

"I'm off to paint something that wants me to paint it, instead of this canvas that doesn't want me to paint it." Charlotte grinned and walked away with a wave of her hand.

That afternoon, Noah and Jay attacked the job of building the ramp. Sara helped when she could, jealous of Charlotte's skill with a saw and quick job of measuring boards for the guys. She measured and cut them, and Noah and Jay efficiently put them together.

Cooper sat in the shade watching all of

them until he spotted some birds on the beach and went chasing after them. Charlotte laughed at his antics and snapped some pictures with her cell phone.

Noah jogged to the beach to retrieve the dog, though he hadn't gone far. "Coop, come on." He bent down and patted the dog, then threw a piece of driftwood. Coop went charging down the beach after it.

Charlotte took more photos. "They look so carefree, don't they?"

Sara stood next to her friend. "They do." She was still boggled that Noah had a dog. A pet. But she was beginning to get used to the idea and this new Noah McNeil.

They finished the ramp and Jay left to check on things in the kitchen. Charlotte went to paint yet another piece of furniture she'd been working on.

"You guys did a great job." Sara looked at the long sloping ramp. "That should be easy for Aunt Lil to walk up, even with her walker."

"Hope it works for her." He picked up the last of his tools, crossed over to his vehicle, and put them inside.

She wasn't ready for him to leave. Not yet. "Hey, do you want a cold beer? Sit and rest for a bit? Do you have time?" The questions rushed out of her.

He rewarded her with a smile. "I do have time, and I'd love a beer."

He and Coop walked up the ramp and they all went inside. She grabbed a couple of beers and handed them to Noah to unscrew the tops before they returned to the deck.

He sank onto the rocker loveseat and she sat beside him.

"That breeze feels great." He shoved his hand through his hair, then took a sip of his beer.

Cooper settled in the shade by the door, resting his head on his paws and closing his eyes.

"Looks like chasing driftwood is tiring." She nodded toward Cooper.

"A dog's life. Someone's got to do it." He grinned at her.

She had to drag her gaze away from his grinning face. And his twinkling eyes.

How could this be happening? Was she actually smitten with the man again? After all these years?

He watched Sara take a sip of her beer. He watched her lips. And her delicate fingers wrapped about the bottle. And her long eyelashes. She licked her lips after her drink and set the bottle down on the table beside her.

The breeze lifted locks of her hair, framing her face.

He tore his gaze from her and looked out at the sea, taking a long swallow of his beer. As if that was going to calm his jangled nerves. He looked back at her and she was staring right at him.

For a moment, time froze in place. He didn't notice the wind, the waves, the call of the gulls that had been so obvious just moments earlier.

Nothing existed but Sara and him.

She licked her lips again with a small dart of her tongue, and that was it. He took in a deep breath of air and set his beer on the table.

As if in slow motion, he reached out to touch her face, trailing his finger along her jawline.

She sat still, her gaze locked on his face.

He lowered his lips toward hers and gently, ever so gently, kissed those lips. An electric shock jolted through him. She raised a hand to cling to his arm. He kissed her again, lost in the sigh that escaped her lips.

He pulled back and looked at her flushed face. She opened her eyes, shining with emotion.

"I've waited a very long time for that. Never thought it would happen again." He fought to get his words out past the emotions that threatened to choke him.

"It was... I never thought..." She let out another sigh. "I'm glad you moved to Belle Island and we..." She shook her head. "I can't even get my thoughts untangled."

He reached out and cradled her face with his hand. "I know that feeling." His own thoughts and feelings were crashing against each other like waves on the sand.

He draped an arm around her and pulled her close, pressing a quick kiss to the top of her head. She dropped a hand on his leg, the touch searing him.

They sat like that, not talking, watching the world go by around them. People walking past them on the beach, pelicans flying overhead, and Cooper snoring gently beside them. But none of that seemed to pierce the magic wrapped around them.

CHAPTER 23

Friday raced by in a whirl of activity for Sara. She cleaned Aunt Lil's room and put on fresh sheets. She shopped for all of Aunt Lil's favorite foods. The whole time she worked, her mind replayed last night over and over.

Noah had stayed until the sun set. They'd talked and kissed. His kisses had stirred long-buried feelings. Feelings she'd hidden for so many years. Now they swirled around her and memories popped into her mind at every turn.

Noah McNeil had reentered her life like a storm surge, sweeping along everything in its path. Every emotion, every memory.

This was not what she'd expected on this trip back to Belle Island. Not at all. She gathered a load of laundry, and as she walked past the sunroom she peered through the glass doors and noticed the easel. There was paint on the canvas. Charlotte had started painting. Fabulous news.

She hummed as she went about her chores. Every part of her thrummed with life and happiness. Aunt Lil was better and coming home. She had her two best friends here with her.

And Noah. Noah McNeil was back in her life.

She grabbed the towels from the dryer and buried her face in their fresh, clean scent. She dumped them into the clothes basket and loaded the dryer with another load.

She'd get this load folded then go and see if Jay needed any help in the kitchen.

She found him there working with a new cook he'd found to help out. Jay was patiently showing the worker how to make their famous cinnamon rolls. He looked up and shrugged at her as if saying this was going to take longer than he thought. But Jay did need help in the kitchen. He couldn't be in it twenty-four seven, and Aunt Lil wouldn't be up to helping out like she had before. Not for a while anyway.

"Can I do anything for you?"

"Could you get the tables set for the dinner rush?" Jay sighed. "I'm a bit behind."

"I can do that."

"The silverware needs to be rolled in napkins, then placed on the tables. There's an order of fresh flowers I haven't gotten into the vases yet, either."

"I'm on it." Finally, some chores she could do. How much could she screw up napkin rolls and flowers?

She rolled the silverware and placed it around on the tables. Then she tackled the flowers. Not as easy as she'd thought as she wrestled the stems into vases and messed with each one until she thought it looked right. Okay, maybe flower arranging wasn't her forte either. If Diane fired her, she definitely wouldn't take a job in a flower shop...

"Hey, you."

She looked up to see Noah standing in the doorway. A rush of emotion flooded through her and she broke a stem on one of the flowers she was holding. "Oops."

"Here, let me help with those."

"You know how to arrange flowers?"

"Of course. We get them in often for events at the community center."

"Well then, you can finish these up while I place the ones I already fought with on the tables."

They finished up the task and she looked around the dining room. Everything looked perfect and ready to go.

Jay poked his head out of the kitchen. "Hey, Sara, a server called in sick. I don't suppose you'd like to help wait tables tonight."

"Of course, I will." That was something she was good at. She'd grown up helping Aunt Lil in the dining room.

"Thanks."

She didn't know why he was thanking her. It was her job now to help run the inn and help Aunt Lil. Especially because she might be on a permanent vacation from her job after her screw up. She'd sent in her official notice for taking vacation but had heard nothing back from the agency or Diane. She pushed the thought away and turned back to Noah.

"I was going to ask you out tonight, but it appears you're going to be busy." He had the expression of a kid who'd been told Christmas was delayed.

"Sorry." She'd have loved to go out with him, but helping Aunt Lil came first.

"Well, I guess I'll eat dinner here. That way at least I can see you."

"And I'll be your waitress. But no special attention for you, mister." She grinned.

"Darn." He flashed her an impish grin. "But there is one thing I need from you."

"What's that?"

He glanced around the room, then reached over and pulled her close. "A kiss."

Then she lost all thought of chores and helping and everything else when Noah's lips closed on hers.

CHAPTER 24

Sara went to pick up Aunt Lil the next morning. Aunt Lil was sitting by the front door of the rehab center with Ashley, waiting for her.

"There you are." Aunt Lil glanced at her watch.

"I'm early," Sara insisted.

"I'm anxious to get home. I've had enough of hospitals and rehab." She turned to Ashley. "Not that you didn't take excellent care of me."

"Remember what I said and take it easy."

"I'll make sure she does." Sara turned to her aunt. "You will take it easy. I'm going to make sure of it."

"I'm feeling fine now. There's a lot I can do even with this silly walker Ashely insists I use."

They got Aunt Lil settled in the car.

"I'm going to stop by the inn and check on you." Ashley closed the car door.

"Don't you have other patients to take care of? I'm fine."

"Thanks, Ashley, for everything you've done for Aunt Lil." Sara walked around the car and slipped in.

Ashley waved to them as she pulled away.

When they got back on the island, Aunt Lil's face broke into a smile. "It's so good to be back here."

She pulled around the inn and up to The Nest, laughing when she saw Jay, Robin, and Charlotte waiting for them. "Look at your welcoming committee."

"There's no need to make a fuss. And what's that ramp?"

"So you can get inside. Ashley said no stairs for you for a while."

"That's just silly. I can do stairs."

"Aunt Lil, do not argue with me. I'm going to hover around and drive you crazy and make sure you take things slowly."

Aunt Lil rolled her eyes. "Well, that sounds like fun for both of us."

Jay opened the car door and reached in his

hands for Aunt Lil to take. He carefully helped her out of the car, grabbed her walker from the back seat, and handed it to her.

"I really don't need that."

"I'm sure you don't, but let's use it for a while, anyway." He stood by her side as she maneuvered her way up the ramp.

She hugged Robin and Charlotte as she got up to them. "It's so good to see you girls. I hope you've been keeping Sara company."

"It's been great having her back home." Robin opened the door for Aunt Lil.

Aunt Lil went inside and looked around. "Oh, it's so good to be home in my own space."

Sara thought Aunt Lil looked tired from all the commotion. "Do you want to nap for a bit? Or at least sit?"

Aunt Lil turned to her and gave her a stern look. "Do not treat me like an invalid. I won't have it."

She grinned. There was the old spirited Aunt Lil she knew and loved. "Yes, Ma'am."

"Now I'm going to go sit in my recliner. Jay, could you bring in my suitcase and put it in my room? And how about some tea for everyone? Sara, can you make some?"

"I've got the tea already made." Charlotte walked into the kitchen.

They all sat and laughed and drank tea and Sara felt at home, at peace. The only thing missing was Noah.

Sara threw herself into helping at the inn and taking care of Aunt Lil. And by taking care of Aunt Lil, she meant trying to keep her aunt from overdoing it. Aunt Lil was sitting in her office by the first day, sorting through paperwork with Robin. Robin insisted she could still do the ordering and talked to Lil about getting a newer software system for running the inn, which Aunt Lil agreed to look into.

By the next day, she took a couple short stints at the reception desk. Then she insisted on helping in the kitchen, but Jay sat her at a table and gave her apples to peel for pies he was making.

Sara stood in the kitchen, hands on her hips. "You're supposed to be taking it easy."

"I am. See? I'm sitting down."

But Sara could see the tiredness and a bit of pain in her aunt's eyes. "After this, you're going back to The Nest. I'm going to make you dinner and you're going to rest."

"You're cooking?" Jay eyed her.

Sara grinned. "Well, by me cooking, I meant I would grab some food from you and Lil and I will eat it at The Nest where's it's quiet and she can't pop up and work."

"Great idea." Jay nodded.

"I'm fine. Quit hovering," Aunt Lil insisted.

"Please?" Sara wasn't above begging.

"I'm going to finish up these apples first."

"I'll help." Sara sat beside her aunt. She managed to peel one apple for every three Aunt Lil peeled.

Once they finished the chore, Aunt Lil stood up slowly. Sara handed her the walker and her aunt sighed. "Don't really need that thing."

"Humor me."

They slowly walked the distance through the dining room, through the inn, and down the hall to their private wing. Sara was fairly certain this wasn't what Ashley had meant when she said short walks…

When they got to The Nest, Aunt Lil settled into her recliner. "Oh, Sara, can you hand me my e-reader? I'm in the middle of a great series."

Sara handed her the reader and the teal throw from the back of the couch. "Now if I go check on how the yellow cottage is coming along, will you stay there and rest?"

Aunt Lil rolled her eyes. "Don't you have a job to get back to in Boston?"

Good question. Did she? But she just sent her aunt a glare. "I'll be back later and I'll bring our supper."

Sara walked out the back door, down the ramp, and around the corner. As she passed the sunroom, she glanced inside. Charlotte was standing in front of the easel, paintbrush in hand, working on her painting.

Perfect. Hopefully, she was finding her mojo again.

Things were coming together nicely. The teal cottage was ready for guests. The yellow cottage was at least moving along. Robin had sorted out Aunt Lil's bookwork and was going to help her get set up on a new system. Aunt Lil was doing better than she'd hoped. Charlotte was painting.

And there was Noah. He'd gone to visit Zoe for a few days and she missed him. Which was silly because... well, soon she'd be headed back to Boston. So she shouldn't let herself get involved with Noah.

A few kisses weren't getting involved, right? They were just... friends. Friends who kissed. She rolled her eyes at herself.

Anyway, things on Belle Island were falling into place.

There was that one tiny detail though... did she still have a job or not?

CHAPTER 25

"How'd the interview go?" Zoe slipped into the seat across from Noah at their agreed-upon meeting place, a trendy cafe near her apartment.

"It went well, I guess? I mean, it's been years since I've interviewed anywhere. I kind of fell into the community center job on Belle Island."

"But you'd get to use more of your education with this job, right? More promotion and advertising? You like that, right?"

He did like the advertising business, and he'd enjoyed coming up with promotions for events at the community center. Not that it was anything like coming up with campaigns for their clients at the agency in Boston.

"It would be great to have you near. We

could do a regular once a week dinner out. Try new places around town. We could even hit the theme parks just like when I was a little girl. I loved them."

"You still do, don't you?"

"I do. But I haven't been since I moved here." She leaned forward. "So, did you like the company? I heard they are really expanding. Who knew there were so many retirement communities down here and more of them going up every day."

"It's a competitive business in this area. Well, all of Florida, I guess."

"Did it sound like something you'd enjoy?"

"I think so." But it would be a big change. Instead of knowing most of the people who came to the community center like on Belle Island, he'd be organizing events for the community and promoting them. He'd also be working on creative ideas for promoting the whole retirement center. It would be challenging and a big change from what he did now.

"I hope you get it." Zoe bobbed her head enthusiastically.

He hadn't sorted out how he felt about all of this, so he changed the subject. "Have you made many friends here?"

"Oh, work people. We hang out on Friday nights most weeks."

Maybe she was lonely? Is that why she wanted him near? It had been hard being apart. When she'd gone to college, that had been a big adjustment, but Belle Island had still been her home and she'd come home often. Now she lived near Orlando. Really it was only a few hours away, but… his home was no longer her home. She had her own apartment, job, life. He hadn't been prepared for how hard it had been to let her go…

Zoe looked up at him, her eyes twinkling. "Hey, can we split a dessert, too? They have a dark chocolate cake that sounds heavenly."

He smiled at her. "But of course." He couldn't deny her anything. And he'd even take a new job, away from his beloved Belle Island, if it would make her happy or make her life easier.

The thought of her being up here alone and lonely tore at his heart. Oh, she'd find friends soon enough. She was a personable woman with a charming personality. But maybe this transition was as hard on her as it was for him.

Besides, he'd learned one thing through all of this. Family came first.

~

Sara walked into the sunroom the next day and found Charlotte staring at her easel, her head tilted to one side.

From this angle, she couldn't see what Charlotte had painted. "Hey, mind if I take a look?"

Charlotte stood in front of the painting, considering. "I don't know... I'm just so unsure."

"Come on, let me see it."

Charlotte nodded slowly.

She walked around to the front of the canvas and a small gasp escaped her throat. "Oh, Char... that is... wonderful. How did you capture all that emotion so perfectly?" She stared at a scene with Cooper leaping to catch a piece of driftwood and Noah laughing. The waves rolled in behind them, and the sun filtered through the palm trees scattered at the edge of the beach.

"Do you think so? It's so different from what I've been painting."

"Yes, I think so. It's fabulous."

"I used those photos I took of Cooper and Noah the other day for inspiration."

"Well, I'd say you were inspired. This is just..." She spun around and hugged Charlotte. "This is so... fabulous."

Charlotte grinned. "You said that already."

"And I meant it."

"It just kind of flowed from my brushes. I started and then... it seemed to just appear. I still need to work on where the sun hits the water and add a few more details." She tilted her head to one side, critically appraising the painting. "But..." Her voice was tentative. "I think... I think I like it."

Sara laughed. "You're always the toughest judge of your work."

Charlotte gave her a sheepish grin. "I know."

They both turned at the sound of someone in the doorway.

"Noah." She broke into a spontaneous grin. "You're back."

"I am." He rewarded her with his slow, sexy smile.

"Come see Charlotte's painting."

"No, wait—"

"Come on, let him see it."

Charlotte sighed. "Okay, go ahead."

Noah crossed over, looked at the painting,

and let out a low whistle. "Wow, Charlotte… That's… fabulous."

She and Charlotte laughed. "See, I told you."

"That's me and Cooper from the other day, right?"

"Yes, I took some photos and then kind of merged them into an idea for this painting."

"You're really talented. Your painting just pulls a person into the scene."

Charlotte glowed with his praise.

"Hey, you know what you should do?" Noah stepped back, looking at the painting. "You should show that to Paul Clark. He has a gallery in town. Do you know him?"

"I kind of remember him. Friends with Tally?" Charlotte's face crinkled up in concentration.

Sara turned to Charlotte. "You should do that. Show it to Paul."

"Oh, I don't think I'm ready to show this to a gallery owner. This style is so new to me."

Sara put her hands on her hips. "I think you should. It's…"

"Fabulous?" Charlotte laughed.

"Well, it is."

Lil sat in her recliner, watching Sara closely as she chatted with Noah. Sara and Noah had come to check on her. Everyone was always checking on her. Hovering. Like she was some kind of old lady. Well, she wasn't. She was going to get stronger. She'd already given up the walker for a cane, though she'd had to argue with both Sara and Jay.

She glanced back at Sara and Noah. There was something going on there, she was sure of it. Sara's eyes sparkled when Noah told a story about the youth play at the community center. And she wasn't a fool. She could see the way Noah looked at Sara.

She watched them closely as they talked. She wondered if either of them even realized how they felt about each other.

And how had they become so close in such a short time?

"So how did you meet Noah?" Lil leaned forward in her recliner—*ouch, that didn't work*—and leaned back again.

Sara looked up with an almost guilty look on her face. "Oh, I knew him back in Boston. We… worked together."

"Is that so?" What wasn't Sara telling her? She looked at Noah, trying to read his expression to see if that would clue her in more.

"Then I saw him here on the island. Well, to be honest, Cooper found me."

Lil smiled. "That dog, he's a good one."

"He is." Sara seemed glad to change the subject.

"So, when are you planning on returning to Boston?" Lil enjoyed having her niece here, but she wished the woman would quit hovering and they could go back to how they were before. Without Sara acting like she was going to break. Maybe Sara going back to Boston and getting away for a bit would help things get back to normal between them.

"I'm… not sure."

Lil frowned. Uncertainty creased Sara's brow. "You're not staying because of me, are you? I'm fine now. I appreciate how everyone jumped in and helped while I was gone, but I'm fine. Really."

"It's not that." Sara sighed. "It's just I'm not sure if I have a job or not."

"You lost it because of me?"

"No, I was late for a deadline and then I took some much-needed vacation time." Sara stood and paced the floor. "I needed a break. And I've loved being back on Belle Island."

"But what about that big promotion you were up for? Weren't you hoping for partner?"

"I was. But… we'll see what happens now. I'm going to call my boss tomorrow and sort things out."

"She'd be crazy to let you go." Noah jumped to her defense.

Lil smothered a grin. Yes, that Noah McNeil had it bad for her niece. And she was fairly certain Sara was crazy about him, too.

Noah sat outside with Sara that evening on the deck overlooking the beach. Lil had said she was tired and was heading to her room to read for a bit, then early to bed. She hadn't looked tired though. He was pretty sure Lil was just giving them time alone.

He should tell Sara about his job interview in central Florida, but it didn't seem like the time to bring it up. It didn't really matter, anyway. Sara was leaving soon. All the way back to Boston. It wouldn't really matter if he was on

Belle Island or near Orlando. They'd still be miles and miles apart.

Fate was funny sometimes. He'd lost Sara years ago over some stupid note and a phone message gone astray and too much pride to call her again. Now they'd found each other, but they had very different lives.

But he didn't regret for a moment this time with her. He leaned over, tilted her face up, and kissed her.

She smiled. "What was that for?"

"That was for… I don't know. I'm just glad you're here where I can kiss you whenever I want."

A bubble of laughter escaped her. "And I can kiss you whenever I want."

And she did just that.

CHAPTER 26

R obin rushed across the entrance area of the inn and grabbed Sara's arm as soon as she entered.

"Sara, you're never going to guess who's here at the inn."

"Who?"

"Mr. Windsor. Mr. *Lyle* Windsor."

"No, really?" Sara darted her eyes, looking for him.

"Yes, he was talking to the group he was with when he checked in. They were talking about Coastal Furniture. And he put the rooms on a Coastal Furniture credit card. I saw it when Lil was checking them in. They're having some kind of small sales meeting here. He reserved one of the meeting rooms."

"Wow, that's some kind of coincidence."

"No, it's not coincidence, it's serendipity. It's fate." Robin threw her arms wide in enthusiasm. "You should go talk to him and pitch your idea."

"I couldn't do that…"

"Why not? You said it was a good idea. And I heard them talking about still looking for an agency. It's amazing the things you can hear just hanging out at the reception desk." Robin grinned.

"You know what? I *am* going to talk to him. It was a good idea even if Diane didn't bother to look at it."

"Atta girl." Robin shoved her in the direction of the dining room. "I happen to know he went in there to grab something to eat."

Sara took a deep breath and started over to the dining room. She glanced back at Robin. Her friend gave her a shooing motion.

She could do this. She could. She walked confidently into the dining room and her gaze swept the room.

There he was, sitting with two other men. Should she interrupt their meal? She could at least ask to meet with him later. The worst that he could say was no.

She strode across the room cloaked in her best all-business ambience. "Mr. Windsor."

He looked at her and frowned. "You're... you're with Diane's company, right?"

Well, she sure didn't know how to answer that question. "I did present an idea to you earlier this month."

"I met with her again, but I'm afraid the idea she presented just wasn't original enough."

She squared her shoulders and jumped off the cliff. "I've come up with an idea that I believe is unique and a great fit for your company. If you'd have some time while you're here, I'd love to present it to you."

He looked at her and frowned again. "Did Diane track me down here and send you to pitch again?"

She shook her head. "No, I'm here visiting my aunt. She owns the inn."

"Your aunt is Lillian?"

She nodded.

"Was sorry to hear about her fall. Nasty thing. I'm glad she's up and about some now."

"You know her?"

"I do. I've been bringing my family here for vacation for the last six years or so. Decided it was also a great place for a sales meeting for my senior staff. My family is coming down at the end of the week and we'll stay for a few days." He stared at her a bit longer. "Yes, I'll hear your idea. How would late afternoon work? We have meetings scheduled after lunch, but I could see you about four."

"Four works for me." Any time he could have thrown out there worked for her. "I'll see you then. Meet you in the lobby?"

"See you then."

Sara turned and walked away, doing her best not to skip with joy. Ha, she still had a chance to pitch her idea.

Take that, Terrence.

Take that, Diane.

She couldn't wipe the triumphant smile from her face.

That evening Noah and Sara walked along the water's edge, headed to Lighthouse Point to watch the sunset.

"And then I talked to Windsor and pitched my idea and he loved it. Absolutely thrilled with it." She did a little dance and whirled around.

"No surprise. You always came up with the best ideas." Noah took her hand, and they continued down the beach. "Now what happens?"

She shrugged. "I'm not sure. I was honest and told him I wasn't sure where I stood with the agency right now, but that I'd call in the morning and clear that up. He said he wanted the idea, anyway. But that would get messy if I'm getting let go, because I already turned the idea in to Diane."

"You sure aren't doing this the easy way, are you?" He grinned.

"Nope, not at all. I'm going to call Diane in the morning. I'm hoping the good news about Windsor will ease her anger a bit."

"They're quite the catch for a client. I'm sure she'll be thrilled."

"I guess we'll find out."

They continued their walk until they reached the lighthouse and sank onto the sand. She leaned against him. They sat and watched the sky burst into streaks of purple and orange.

"That's beautiful," she whispered.

"I never tire of this island's sunsets."

"I'll miss them when I go back to Boston."

"I'll miss *you* when you go back to Boston." He lifted her hand up and pressed his lips against it.

Warmth surged through her along with an ache of loneliness.

There it was.

She was leaving and heading back to her life. He had his life here.

He pressed a kiss against the side of her forehead and turned to look out at the sea.

She wanted to tell him she'd miss him, too.

Tell him… tell him…

… that she was falling for him all over again. Or maybe, just maybe, the feelings had never really gone away.

But she sat beside him in silence, unable to find the words.

CHAPTER 27

Sara paced back and forth in The Nest the next morning, working up the nerve to call Diane. Really, why was she letting the woman intimidate her? And she'd earned the vacation days she was using now. *And* she'd offered to work remotely instead of taking vacation if Diane needed her.

She squared her shoulders. She could do this. She stalked over and snatched the phone from the counter. It rang in her hand and she almost dropped it in surprise. She fumbled with it and slipped her finger across it to answer.

"Sara, it's Diane."

She swallowed. Then swallowed again. "Morning, Diane." She tried to make her voice sound nonchalant.

"I was really disappointed when you missed your deadline."

"I know, I'm sorry, but—"

Diane cut her off. "But I understood. You were with your aunt. Well, I didn't really understand because I have no family. But I know she's important to you."

Sara walked over and plopped down on the chair, surprise crashing over her.

"And to be honest, your pitch impressed me. I was impressed that you... showed some backbone standing up and insisting your idea was good—it was, by the way. I did go and read your proposal after you insisted it was one of your better ideas. You were right. It was brilliant. I only wish I'd read it before I went with Terrence's idea. His ideas are always efficient and doable, but not very creative."

She pulled the cell away from her ear for a moment, staring at it, not sure she was hearing Diane correctly.

"And you asked for and took what you needed. Time off to be with your Aunt. You've become quite a strong woman in the years you've been with the agency. I think it's about time you were made a partner."

She shot up out of the chair, struggling to

hold on to the phone, and pumped her fist. Yes. Yes!

"Is that something you're interested in?"

She calmed herself. "Yes, it is."

"We can discuss the details when you get back to Boston. Will another week give you enough time?"

"Yes, another week will work for me. I'll be back in the office mid-next week."

"Perfect."

"Thanks, Diane."

Diane ended the call. She stood and stared at her phone. What just happened? Had Diane *complimented* her? *And* offered her the partnership? It was everything she'd been working for, everything she wanted.

She couldn't wait to go tell Aunt Lil, and Robin, and Charlotte... and Noah. She frowned. Noah would be happy for her, she was sure of that.

But taking the partnership would mean lots of long hours and limited time to come back to Belle Island to visit. Though she swore she would make it a priority. No long stretches of time without coming back to visit Aunt Lil.

And would she be visiting Noah? And as what? A friend?

How did getting this promotion—that she'd been working toward for years—make her life so complicated now?

Oh snap, in the excitement she hadn't even told Diane that Windsor had loved her idea. She'd have to email her.

After she went to tell her good news.

Noah walked Cooper on the beach, disappointed they didn't run into Sara this morning. "Sorry, Coop. Looks like our friend isn't out walking today."

Cooper looked up at him with his wise eyes.

"I know, I know. I said friend. And she's becoming something… more."

Cooper cocked his head to one side and Noah could swear the dog understood every word.

"Okay, okay. I care about her. I care about her a lot." He turned and looked out at the sea. "A whole lot."

He ruffled the fur on the back of Cooper's neck. The dog stared at him as if asking what he was going to do about it.

Noah laughed. "Okay, you win. I'm going to

go over to talk to her this evening. Tell her how I feel. I'm going to tell her I'm falling in love with her. Again."

Cooper barked.

Noah reached down and picked up a shell. "A wish would be good about now, huh, Coop?"

The dog barked again.

Noah looked out at the sea, then squeezed his eyes shut for a moment. "I wish that Sara feels the same way about me." He opened his eyes and threw the shell out into the water.

"Let's see how well the lighthouse legend is going to work for us this time, Coop."

He and Cooper headed back down the beach while his mind rushed through trying to find the right words to tell Sara how he felt about her.

Sara threw her arms out and whirled around when she entered the kitchen and found Robin, Charlotte, Aunt Lil, and Jay sipping on coffee.

"Guess what?" She whirled again.

"Haven't seen you do that since you were a young girl. So what's the news?" Aunt Lil looked up from where she was resting on a chair.

"I got the promotion. They offered me partner."

Robin smiled. "Well, that's good news." But her voice didn't sound that enthusiastic.

"That's nice, dear. I know you really worked hard for it." But Sara didn't miss the hint of sadness in Aunt Lil's eyes.

"Char?" She turned to her friend.

"That's great. Really it is. It's just... Robin and I were talking, and we've just decided to find a place to live here. Together. I'm going to let my apartment go in California. I mean, I can paint anywhere, right? I can still fly back if I do get a gallery showing there. I just... missed the island." She shrugged. "I was kind of hoping that you would get fired and stay here with us. The three of us together again."

"Really, you wanted me to get fired?"

Charlotte sighed. "No, I guess not. But selfishly I wanted you to stay here with us."

"You two girls stay in the yellow cottage as long as you want. You wouldn't let me pay you for all the work you've done, so it's the least I can do. And don't argue with me." Aunt Lil eyed Robin. "Especially you. You won't win this time."

Robin laughed. "Okay, okay. But I'm sure

I'll find a job soon and we'll look for an apartment or small house to rent."

"You're not working at Marvin's Sporting Goods?"

"No, Marvin sold it and it's closing. The buyer is combining it with another shop on the mainland."

"Perfect." Aunt Lil grabbed the edge of the counter and got to her feet. "How would you like to come work at the inn? I need someone to set up the software, help with the books, help with managing the staff. You've been wonderful with all you've done. I've been wanting to hire a manager. How about it?"

"I… yes." Robin rushed over and hugged Lil. "I'd love to work for you. You know how much I love this inn."

Sara glanced over at Jay and saw he had a big smile on his face. He turned away and nonchalantly stirred a pot on the stove when he caught her staring at him.

Sara looked around the room. Everyone's life was falling into place. All the people she loved were right here. They would all be here on the island.

And she'd be across the country, miles away.

Everyone she cared about would be here…

CHAPTER 28

Noah looked up from his desk at the community center and smiled when he saw Sara standing there. Maybe his thoughts of needing to talk to her had pulled her here to see him.

He jumped up, walked around the desk, and pressed a quick kiss on her cheek. "This is a nice surprise. What brings you here?"

"I have news."

"What kind of news?" He had news to tell her too. How he felt. But he'd let her go first. He took her hand, led her over to two chairs, and they sat across from each other, knees touching. He took both her hands in his.

She looked at him, her eyes filled with excitement. "I… I got the partnership."

He automatically plastered a smile on his face, because he knew that was the right reaction, even though he didn't feel it. Oh, he was happy for her. She'd worked long and hard for this promotion. But it meant she was leaving the island. Leaving him. He resolutely widened the smile and squeezed her hands. "Well, that *is* good news. Congratulations."

"I thought for sure I'd lost it after I missed that deadline and took all this vacation... but Diane *complimented* me."

"Really? That's a rarity."

"I know." Sara jumped up. "I can't believe I finally, *finally* got offered partner."

He kept the smile frozen on his face. "It's well deserved."

"I feel like I've been working almost my whole adult life just for this. And I finally achieved my goal."

"I hope it makes you very happy, Sara, I do." He stood and walked around behind his desk, needing a bit of distance, needing to think before he spoke the wrong words. Thankful he hadn't blurted out his feelings to her, because she needed nothing standing in her way. *He* wouldn't stand in her way. She could take the promotion, move back to Boston, and just remember their brief time together again with fond memories.

"That's great news. Great." He sat down at his desk. "I… I should get back to work."

"Will I see you later?" Her eyes questioned him.

"Sure. Probably. I have a thing tonight that might keep me tied up." The only thing he had on his schedule tonight was to go over and tell Sara how he felt about her. But his timing was lousy. No way he could tell her now. She'd gotten her dream job, and he wasn't going to stand in her way or complicate her decision.

"Okay, I'll go then. Just wanted to share the news."

He didn't miss the slight hurt that lingered around her eyes. But it was better this way. It was. She disappeared out of his office and he leaned back in his chair, sadness swirling around him. All his excitement from this morning, when he'd finally sorted out his feelings for her and admitted he cared about her dwindled away in the sadness.

His phone rang, and he almost ignored it, but he sighed and answered it.

"Noah, this is Victor from Sunshine Communities. Listen, we've talked it over and we'd like to offer you the position. We'll beat your salary you have now by a third. And our benefits are top-notch. Do you think you're interested in the position?"

"I'll take it." He said the words quickly, automatically, before he could think it through. That's just what he needed. A change. A new job. He'd be closer to Zoe, and she seemed to want that.

"That's excellent. We'll send you the employment papers to sign."

He clicked off his phone and looked around his office. Just like that, he'd made a leap. A change.

He was going to leave Belle Island.

He called Zoe and left a voice message telling her the good news…

Sara returned to The Nest early that evening to find Aunt Lil sitting out on the deck, sipping a glass of wine.

"Grab a glass, come join me."

She grabbed a glass and came back to sit. Aunt Lil poured her a drink. "I'm going to miss having you here. Even if you do hover over me too much." Lil smiled.

"I'm going to miss being here."

"You don't have to go, you know. You're always welcome here." A smile teased the corners of Aunt Lil's lips. "If you don't hover."

"But I got the promotion."

"You did." Aunt Lil nodded.

"It's what I've always wanted. I've worked toward it for years."

"Yes. And are you sure that's what will make you happy now?"

"I…" She let out a long breath. "I'm not sure. I've loved being back on the island. I love spending time with you and Robin and Charlotte."

"And Noah?" Aunt Lil looked over the top of her glasses, pinning her with a stare.

"Yes, now there's Noah."

"And you care about him. He cares about you too, you know. I can see it plain as day on his face. The man is smitten with you whether he knows it or not."

"You think so?" He hadn't said a word about his feelings and she had no clue how he felt. How deep his feelings might be. Or even if he had feelings for her anymore. Maybe this was just a brief encounter. Reliving the past. "He hasn't said anything."

"Men are like that sometimes. Slow to realize how they feel and even slower to say something."

"I couldn't just stay here because of Noah…"

"Why not? And would it be just because of him? Or have you enjoyed yourself here? Your life in Boston is busy, busy. You rarely take time off. You don't take vacation. Is that any way to live?" Lil took a sip of her wine. "Sometimes you just need to take a bit of time, sit alone with your thoughts, and enjoy the moment."

"I've done that here the last few weeks. And spent time with Char and Robin. I've enjoyed that, too. Talking with them. Laughing with them." She looked down at the burgundy-colored liquid in her glass and swirled it around. "I've had… fun."

Aunt Lil smiled. "So you just have to choose what kind of life you want. Only you can decide that."

"I wouldn't even have a job if I stayed here."

"You could work here at the inn, or you could open your own agency. You could do anything you want. You've got great ideas and are very creative. I'm sure the businesses around here could use help with promotion. And there's this thing called computers. I've heard a person can work from anywhere." Lil grinned.

"I just don't know…"

"Only you can figure that out."

Sara put her glass down. "You know, I think I might go take a walk. Think for a bit."

"That's a good idea."

Sara wound her way down the ramp and out onto the cooling sand. With a brief wave to Aunt Lil, she turned and headed toward the lighthouse.

Lil watched Sara walk down the beach. Oh, to be young and foolish again. Because her niece was being foolish. She had a chance at real happiness.

Lil was certain that real happiness for Sara wasn't going to be found at a job in Boston with endless hours and nothing much else in her life.

But it was Sara's decision to make. No one could make those hard decisions in life for you. Sometimes the fates decided to force you into making the tough choices.

Like when she'd taken custody of Sara all those years ago. Oh, she hadn't really had a choice—there was no one else. But she'd been so frightened of that little girl with the wide eyes filled with tears.

But they'd made a good life for themselves. A duo against the world. It had taken time, but Sara had finally lost the haunted look in her eyes. She'd made friends with Robin and Charlotte, and the three of them had filled The Nest with laughter.

She pushed off of her chair, steadying herself before she took a step, and walked over to the railing, looking out at the sea.

The salty air refreshed her, invigorated her. The island was in her very bones. She smiled then at the thought. Maybe the island in her bones would get to speeding up the healing of her fracture and life could get back to the way it was.

Sara got smaller and smaller in the distance. There was nothing she could do at this point to help her niece. She'd suggested Sara think about what she really wanted out of life. No one but Sara could make that decision.

She clasped the railing. Who knew that

raising a child was this hard? Even after the child became an adult.

Sara hadn't gotten halfway to the lighthouse before she knew what she wanted. She was certain. More certain than she'd been about anything in a very long time. She crossed over to a stand of palm trees, out of the wind. She slipped her phone out of her pocket and called Diane.

"Yes?"

"Diane, it's Sara."

"Calling to say you're coming back sooner, I hope?"

"No, actually… I'm calling to say I'm turning down your offer of partner. And I'll be sending in a letter of resignation."

"You're what?" Diane's crisp voice cut through the airways.

"I've decided that I'm going to stay here on the island."

"But you've worked for years for this position."

"I have. But… things change. What I want from life has changed. I don't want my whole life to be about work. I have family here. Friends here." And someone she loved here. Loved very much. She just needed to go find him and tell him.

"Are you certain? Chances like this don't come along every day."

"I'm certain. Oh, and another thing. I got you the Coastal Furniture account."

"What?" It was hard to miss the surprise in Diane's voice.

"Windsor was here at my aunt's inn. I pitched my idea, and he loved it. I'll have him contact you and you can work out the details with him."

"That's... wonderful. You did a great job. Thank you." Diane paused. "We're going to miss you here."

"Thank you." *She* wasn't going to miss the long hours. Nor the crazy demands. Nor the traffic.

She would have night skies filled with stars, salty air, walks on the beach, Aunt Lil, her friends... and if everything worked out, she'd have Noah back in her life again.

"I'll send in my official resignation. Bye, Diane." She put her phone back in her pocket and raced down toward the water, whirling in a crazy circle. She hurried up the beach and touched the wind-beaten stone on the lighthouse. "Hello, old friend. Looks like I'll be coming to visit you more often."

She wandered down to the edge of the water, letting the waves lap over her feet and slip back into the sea.

A light purple shell tumbled in the water and stopped by her feet when the next wave rolled away. She reached down and picked it up. She rubbed it with her fingers and smiled.

She closed her eyes and made her wish. With all her hopes and possibilities stretching before her, she tossed the shell out into the water.

CHAPTER 29

Noah saw Sara standing alone out on the point, watching the sunset. "Hey, Cooper, this isn't good. I told her I had *a thing* tonight."

Coop looked up at him.

"We should just turn around before she sees us."

Coop looked down the beach and then back at him. Then he took off at a dead run, racing toward Sara.

"Great, just great." He whistled, but Coop ignored him. With a sigh, he jogged after the dog. The very disobedient dog. Maybe he should take him to obedience classes...

Well, he could tell her about his new job...

Sara had dropped to her knees, her arms

wrapped around Cooper. She smiled up at him when he got close. Not too close. He carefully kept his distance.

"Hey, there. Cooper needed a walk." As if to explain why he was so very, very busy tonight and couldn't come see her.

She stood. "I have news."

"You already told me, remember? And now I have news."

She tilted her head. "You do?"

"Yes, so I'll go first." He raked his hand through his hair. "I've taken a new job. I'm leaving Belle Island and moving close to Zoe. It's a great job. More responsibility. More money. It was time for a change."

A look of surprise crossed her face. "You're leaving Belle Island?"

"I am. Zoe wants me nearer and... well, I'd do anything for her. It will be nice to be closer and see her more often. I miss her."

"That sounds like it will work out for both of you then."

Noah got the feeling that she wasn't that thrilled for him. But maybe it just didn't matter to her where he lived. "So, that's my news. What's yours?"

"Oh..." She turned and looked out at the

sea. "My news." She turned back to him with a small smile. "My news. Um, oh, it's not really my news. It's more Robin's news. She took a job working as a manager at the inn."

"That will make it easier for you to leave, I bet. Knowing Robin's here helping with the inn."

"Yes. Easier to leave." She reached down and petted Cooper. "I've got to get back. I'm meeting Robin and Char for a drink on the deck. I'll let you finish your walk."

He nodded.

She gave him one more long look and he just couldn't get a read on it. She turned and walked away. She looked sad, maybe. Disappointed? Maybe she hoped to see him some when she came back to visit her aunt. But he wasn't much interested in some superficial long-distance relationship. Besides, he knew that once she got back to Boston and threw herself into being partner, her trips back to the island would be few and far between.

"Come on, Coop." He headed in the opposite direction of the inn and didn't turn back even once to watch her walk away.

"Seriously, Sara. You are so stubborn sometimes." Robin glared at her in the low light from the solar lantern on the deck.

"Robin's right. You are." Charlotte nodded. "You should have told him how you felt. That you turned down the promotion and you're staying."

"I couldn't. He's moving, and he wants to be closer to his niece. *She's* what's important to him. His number one responsibility." Sara took a sip of her wine. "And he sounded excited about a new challenge with the new job, and it's more money."

"But if he knew how you felt—"

She lifted her hand to cut off Robin. "No, he wants to be near Zoe. He takes his responsibility for her very seriously. She's his family. I'm not going to throw any complications into his decisions."

"You're making a mistake." Charlotte shook her head.

"I'm not. I'm giving him the freedom to move and not worry about how I feel. I don't want to become another of his responsibilities or have him feel guilty about moving. Besides, he's never said a word to me about his feelings." She looked at Robin, then Charlotte. "And neither of you say a word to him about me staying either. He doesn't need to know."

"Mistake, Sara. Really big." Robin stretched her hands out in front of her.

"But it's mine to make." She took a sip of her wine and looked out at the gulf. Sadness wrapped around her. She was happy she was staying and still believed she'd made the right decision to turn down the promotion to partner. That life in Boston just didn't appeal to her anymore.

She'd find work here and be near to help Aunt Lil.

"At least the three of us will all be together again." Charlotte raised her glass.

They clinked glasses.

"To the three of us together again." Sara smiled at her friends, but the sadness still lingered at the edge of her mind.

CHAPTER 30

Noah got back from his morning walk with Cooper to find Zoe sitting on his front step. "Zoe, what are you doing here?"

"I came to talk to you."

"Is something wrong?"

"I could ask the same thing."

He dropped to the step beside her. "Why do you say that?"

"First off, since when do you make a snap decision to take a new job? My *real* uncle would have called me, discussed it, the pros and cons. Like I did when I took my job."

"But—"

"And you didn't sound excited when you called to tell me you took the job. Something's not right. You know you can't hide things from me. You can't even keep secrets about presents you buy me."

He smiled. Too true. Christmases were *hard*, trying to keep surprises from her.

"So, why don't you talk to me and tell me what's going on?"

"I thought you'd be excited that we'd be near each other again."

"I am. I miss that. But I don't want you taking a job close to me thinking you still need to take care of me."

"But I thought you wanted me closer."

She rolled her eyes at him. "Sometimes you are just so… You should do what *you* want. Stay here if it makes you happy. I just thought you were so lonely without me here. I felt guilty for leaving you. So I thought maybe you wanted to move closer and then I could… I don't know… take care of you for a change."

"But I thought—"

"You don't really want to leave the island, do you?"

He sighed. "Not really."

"You love your job at the community center and all the people there."

"But you're not here."

"I'm not far. And one more thing." She

narrowed her eyes. "Lisa said that you're dating someone. Why didn't you say anything to me?"

"How did she know?"

"Uncle Noah, duh. Small town. And Lisa knows everything. She ran into Tally who mentioned it. You're dating Lil's niece, Sara."

He grinned. "Well, I kind of was. She was a woman I dated back in Boston before…"

"Before Mom and Dad died and you came to take care of me? And I take it she wasn't interested in dating an insta-dad?"

"No, actually, she didn't know why I left. A mix-up with communication."

"And now she's here on the island?"

"But she's leaving. Headed back to Boston for a big new promotion. She made partner in the ad firm I used to work for."

"But you care about her still. I can see that."

He laughed. "You have always been able to read me like a book."

"Came in handy when I was trying to get my way growing up." She grinned. "But… have you told her how you feel? You're not very big on expressing your feelings, you know."

"No, I didn't tell her. She's worked her whole career to get to this partner position. I didn't want to complicate things."

Zoe rolled her eyes again. "Men. Sometimes I think you're a separate species. Why don't you tell her how you feel? Let her make her own decisions?"

"I—" He looked at Cooper staring him, wagging his tail as if agreeing with Zoe. He turned to Zoe. "How'd you get so smart?"

"I had a fabulous uncle who did a great job raising me."

"I love you, Zoe." He leaned over and kissed her cheek.

"Love you, too." Zoe stood. "Now I'm taking Cooper and we're going to go find Lisa and you're going to go find Sara."

He jumped up. "I am."

He watched Zoe and Cooper walk away and pulled out his phone. He called Sara, but she didn't answer. He left a message that he needed to see her.

Then he sent a text message.

Then he called Robin and told her he was looking for Sara.

But just to be certain, he also sent an email to Sara for good measure.

There would not be any lost messages this time.

CHAPTER 31

Sara stood by the lighthouse trying to dispel the overwhelming sadness. It was silly, really. She was going to stay on the island. The island she loved. She hadn't realized how much she missed it until this longer trip home. The island was part of her.

So why couldn't she shake the melancholy?

"I thought I might find you here."

Sara turned around at the sound of Noah's voice. Her heart skipped a beat and her pulse quickened.

"You said you always come to the lighthouse when you're thinking about things."

She nodded. "I—I do."

"I left you a message that I wanted to talk to you."

"I didn't bring my phone…"

"I also texted you, sent an email, and left a message with Robin."

She laughed. "I'm sure I would have gotten at least one of those."

"It was *important* that I see you, and I was taking no chances with lost messages this time."

She looked up into his eyes, uncertain of what was left for him to say. Different paths. Life was always leading them down different paths. She shrugged. "Well, I'm here, what did you want?"

"Sara Wren…" He reached out and took her hands in his.

Instant electricity surged through her, and she grasped his hands in spite of her best intentions to keep her distance.

He paused and looked into her eyes and quite possibly into her soul. "I have fallen in love with you, Sara. Again. Or maybe I never fell out of love. I should have told you how I felt all those years ago, but I never got up the nerve. And now I know my timing is terrible because you're leaving for Boston. But I just had to let you know how I feel."

"Noah, I—"

"Let me finish." He lightly touched her lips,

then brushed a wayward wisp of hair out of her eyes. "I know it will be hard to do this long-distance, but I'd really like to give it a try."

She looked at him, her pulse racing like the waves rushing the shore. "But I don't want a long-distance relationship." The crestfallen look on his face made her hurry to continue. "Because, you see, I ended up turning down the partnership. I'm staying on Belle Island."

He grabbed her and swung her around, her feet flying, her arms wrapped around his neck. "That is the best news I think I've ever heard," he finally said when he set her down.

"And one more thing." She looked up at him, her heart pounding and the lingering sadness swept firmly out to sea.

"What's that?"

"I love you, too, Noah McNeil."

He broke into a wide grin and kissed her again. When he finally pulled away, she asked him, "So... what was that wish you made at Lighthouse Point that first time we were here?"

He dipped his head, then looked at her with an impish grin. "I wished for a kiss from you."

"Ah, I think we can make that wish come true."

She stood on tiptoe and kissed him and he

deepened the kiss. Then he broke away and swung her around again.

"I love you, Sara Wren. You've made me the happiest man on the island."

Sara and Noah walked back to the inn, hand in hand. As they climbed the stairs to the inn, Sara spotted a group of people sitting at the end of the long deck. Aunt Lil, Robin and Charlotte, Jay, and a young woman she believed was Zoe. She waved.

"Look, everyone's here. Let's go tell them the news."

They walked over to the group. Aunt Lil smiled knowingly. Robin and Charlotte had self-satisfied looks on their faces.

"Sara, I'd like you to meet Zoe." Noah reached out a hand and the young woman came and took it.

"I'm glad to see Uncle Noah went and found you." She looked at him and back to Sara. "And did the two of you have a nice talk?"

Noah laughed. "Yes, we did. And I told her I loved her."

"About time the two of you realized it." Aunt Lil bobbed her head.

"So I guess this means you're turning down the job by me and you're staying on the island? Because I just heard Sara is staying."

Noah laughed. A sound that brought such joy to her. Noah's laugh.

"Yes, I'm staying here."

"Perfect." Zoe grinned and hip-checked Noah. "Now you can be someone else's problem." But the adoration for her uncle was evident in her eyes.

"Oh, here's your phone." Robin handed it to her. "There seems to be a lot of messages. Oh, and I have a message from Noah. He's looking for you." Robin grinned.

She laughed when she took the phone. It rang as she took it, and she glanced at the screen. "It's Diane."

"Answer it and tell her you're still sure with your decision," Robin suggested.

"Hello?" She listened to Diane talk while everyone watched her. "Okay, give me some time. I'll think about it." She clicked off the phone.

"You're not changing your mind, are you?" Charlotte's forehead creased in a frown.

"She offered me consulting work. It seems that Windsor doesn't want to work with Terrence or anyone but me for the Coastal Furniture promotion. I'd work from here and just freelance for her for this client."

"There you have it. Your first gig. You can start your own company right here on the island. Oh, and we expect a discounted rate on a new ad campaign for the inn." Robin grinned. "*And* as manager of the inn, I'm thinking of grabbing a round of mimosas for everyone to celebrate all the good news."

"That's a fabulous idea," Aunt Lil agreed.

Sara stood chatting with everyone, with Noah's arm wrapped firmly around her waist. Her heart swelled with happiness. Everything in her life was dropping neatly into place. Her future shone bright, and her life was filled with family, friends, and love.

Robin returned and passed out the drinks, then raised her glass. "To finding love after all these years."

Noah clinked his glass gently against hers. "To finding love. To realizing I'd found it. And to spending my life with you." He kissed her then, right in front of everyone.

But she didn't care. The world faded away

for a moment and all she could feel was his lips on hers and the joy sweeping through her.

Noah McNeil loved her.

And she loved him right back.

I hope you enjoyed One Simple Wish. If you want to read Charlotte's story try Two of a Kind - Book Two in the Charming Inn series.

And if you missed the Lighthouse Point series you can get book one in that series, Wish Upon a Shell.

Do you want to be the first to know about exclusive promotions, news, giveaways, and new releases? Click here to sign up:

VIP READER SIGNUP

Or join my reader group on Facebook. They're always helping name my characters, see my covers first, and we just generally have a good time.

As always, thanks for reading my stories. I truly appreciate all my readers.

Happy reading,

Kay

THANK YOU for reading my story. I hope you enjoyed it. Sign up for my newsletter to be updated with information on new releases, promotions, give-aways, and newsletter-only surprises. The signup is at my website, kaycorrell.com.

Reviews help other readers find new books. I always appreciate when my readers take time to leave an honest review.

I love to hear from my readers. Feel free to contact me at authorcontact@kaycorrell.com

COMFORT CROSSING ~ THE SERIES

The Shop on Main - Book One

The Memory Box - Book Two

The Christmas Cottage - A Holiday Novella (Book 2.5)

The Letter - Book Three

The Christmas Scarf - A Holiday Novella (Book 3.5)

The Magnolia Cafe - Book Four

The Unexpected Wedding - Book Five

The Wedding in the Grove (crossover short story between series - Josephine and Paul from The Letter.)

LIGHTHOUSE POINT ~ THE SERIES

Wish Upon a Shell - Book One

Wedding on the Beach - Book Two

Love at the Lighthouse - Book Three

Cottage near the Point - Book Four

Return to the Island - Book Five

Bungalow by the Bay - Book Six

CHARMING INN ~ Return to Lighthouse Point

COMING IN 2020

One Simple Wish - Book One

Two of a Kind - Book Two

Three Little Things - Book Three

Four Short Weeks - Book Four

Five Years or So - Book Five

SWEET RIVER ~ THE SERIES

A Dream to Believe in - Book One

A Memory to Cherish - Book Two

A Song to Remember - Book Three

A Time to Forgive - Book Four

A Summer of Secrets - Book Five

A Moment in the Moonlight - Book Six

INDIGO BAY ~ Save by getting Kay's complete collection of stories previously published separately in the multi-author Indigo Bay series. The three stories are all interconnected.

Sweet Days by the Bay

Or by them separately:

Sweet Sunrise - Book Three

Sweet Holiday Memories - A short holiday story

Sweet Starlight - Book Nine

ABOUT THE AUTHOR

Kay writes sweet, heartwarming stories that are a cross between women's fiction and contemporary romance. She is known for her charming small towns, quirky townsfolk, and enduring strong friendships between the women in her books.

Kay lives in the Midwest of the U.S. and can often be found out and about with her camera, taking a myriad of photographs which she likes to incorporate into her book covers. When not lost in her writing or photography, she can be found spending time with her ever-supportive husband, knitting, or playing with her puppies —two cavaliers and one naughty but adorable Australian shepherd. Kay and her husband also love to travel. When it comes to vacation time, she is torn between a nice trip to the beach or the mountains—but the mountains only get considered in the summer—she swears she's allergic to snow.

Learn more about Kay and her books at kaycorrell.com

While you're there, sign up for her newsletter to hear about new releases, sales, and giveaways.

WHERE TO FIND ME:
kaycorrell.com
authorcontact@kaycorrell.com

Join my Facebook Reader Group. We have lots of fun and you'll hear about sales and new releases first!
https://www.facebook.com/groups/KayCorrell/

facebook.com/KayCorrellAuthor

instagram.com/kaycorrell

pinterest.com/kaycorrellauthor

amazon.com/author/kaycorrell

bookbub.com/authors/kay-correll